"*David Martin Anderson writes three interconnected stories in 'Les Trois Papillons' (The Three Butterflies) with three main characters: Frederick VonObst's story takes place in 1944, Richard O'Malley's in 1972, and Mitchell Jameson's in 2000. The protagonists' stories coincide with the migration of Old World swallowtail butterflies, a factual migration taking place every 28 years from the South of France to Freiburg in the Black Forest in Germany. The butterflies have no choice but to swarm every 28 years when their population grows unduly large. Will the three men in our story change or perish? Is their fate due to free-will? Or is it pre-determined based on a 28-year cycle?*

Freddie, Richard, and Mitchell's stories connect categorically. The three men are authentic, concerned with honor, and their obligation to life. Their lives involve war-time and family obligations. They each have strong women in their lives who love them and want to help them. The men's characters are strong, and we understand their internal struggles are real and painful. The stories are intricate, intertwining, and fascinating to read.

I rate Les Trois Papillons 4 out of 4 stars, for its unique structure of three stories in one, making one compelling story. It was creative, authentic, and a magic combination of harsh reality and transcendent emotions. There is nothing I disliked; even the harsh reality moments felt like an essential part of the story, but some readers may find them too grim. I recommend this story to people who love war stories, family sagas, love stories, human drama, and exceptional characters."

Online Book Club

Les Trois Papillons

(The Three Butterflies)

A novel by
David Martin Anderson

Use the above QR Code to connect to the author.
DavidMartinAnderson.com

ConRoca Publishing
132 Ridge Trail
Boerne, TX 78006
ConRocaPublishing.com

ISBN 978-1-892617-28-6 (Paperback)
ISBN 978-1-892617-29-3 (Digital)

Printed in the United States of America

10 9 8 7 6 5 4 3 2 1

To Mary,

With Steadfast Love

Author's Note:

Les Trois Papillons is a family saga spanning two countries (Germany and America) over a fifty-six year period. It is a historical fiction that begins at the end of World War II and culminates during the millennium. The plot follows three generations of men whose downward spirals in life correspond to the twenty-eight year cyclical migration of Old World Swallowtail butterflies out of the south of France. The question all three must confront is how much does free will play into their pivotal life-altering decisions or are those decisions predisposed by fate.

Originally written twenty years ago, this novel never gained traction because it was neither short enough to be considered a novella (25,000 word maximum) nor long enough to be considered a full-fledged novel (65,000 word minimum). It fell in the in-between chasm major publishers avoid. Twenty years ago the publishing world existed at the whim of traditional publishing companies with rigid standards. Today, this is no longer the case. Traditional publishing companies are fading away with the emergence of direct publishing and EBooks.

Recently, I have been rewriting a few of my older unheralded stories that I believe have potential for readership. Being a better writer today than twenty years ago, it was easy to throw myself into revamping this one because it drew on personal experiences. Personal experiences can be a driving force in creating a passionate novel. I suppose that is what one tries to do as a writer, draw on experiences both good and bad to create a worthwhile memorable story.

Each chapter of this novel contains three unique stories that ultimately converge in the final chapter. I hope you find Les Trois Papillons much to your liking.

Enjoy!

(1944)

No one knew the exact origin of the butterflies. Some said they took flight from the south of France near the city of Toulon. Others speculated they originated from the rich delta of the Rhone valley. The truth is the place of origin ranked insignificant when compared to the journey. By surviving the journey they became a rarity, arriving once every twenty-eight years, a generation apart from all others. And the ones that persevered and reached their destination did so because of one undeniable axiom—change or perish. For without metamorphosis, they could not begin the journey. Without change they could not bask in the sunlight nor savor the best of the summer days yet to come.

The warm mid-August thermal propelled the swarm of butterflies northward along the western Alps and over the crests of the Jura Mountains. It had been a migration long in the making. As with each prior summer, their population had increased, outstripping what their native habitat could support. By the twenty-eighth year their numbers swelled to the breaking point and forced them onward to a remote meadow hundreds of kilometers away. Like prior broods, only a few would successfully weather the harsh elements and reach the breeding ground deep in the heart of the Black Forest. Most would falter. The tortuous winds would prove too harsh or their gossamer wings too frail. And the natural predators, the swifts and swallows, would deplete the swarm even more. They were, after all, the succulent feasts nourishing their predators' offspring and completing a food chain existing for eons. Yet, the most determined ones would ultimately endure. Pressing onward, following base instincts, they would locate a field hidden in a faraway forest. With their descent into Germany's southwest province, they would rain from heaven and encircle a lush meadow blotting out the sun with their yellow and black wings. Then, with less than a kilometer to go, they would brave one final hurdle to complete their ambitious odyssey, the one imposed by man.

Frederick VonObst hid on the edge of the meadow and crouched low behind a thick spruce. He had been waiting his entire life for the return of Old World Swallowtails. Now, with the flyby moments away, he reflected on this rare migration and sorely realized it had not been his first opportunity to seize the moment. The last time butterflies arrived, circumstances prevented him from being there. Years earlier the Great War conscripted him away. Now, in 1944, he had managed to postpone war long enough to coincide with their arrival. This time he manipulated the outcome *by enlisting*.

As a fifty-two-year-old volunteer for the Führer, he considered himself a patriot in his country's time of need. And he felt relieved for not only was he able to be in the meadow on this most blessed day but he already knew his first assignment. This time he would not be fighting in the trenches of France while dodging machine gun bullets and donning a gas mask. This time he would be garrisoned in Germany behind a cushy desk, only five hours away by train at the secret government post of Bergen-Belsen. No doubt, he would free-up younger men to fight on the battlefield.

Reflecting on the impetuous decision to enlist, he now harbored second thoughts. He had chartered his course based on moral conscience, he told himself. He was doing the right thing, he swore. Nevertheless, he still found this war distasteful. He knew Germany's campaigns were not going well. He had attended far too many students' funerals and the authorities, particularly the Nazi propaganda corps, had lied about the worsening situation, *something the Kaiser never would have done*. His skepticism spawned defeatist thoughts: Why were the Allied bombers able to penetrate air defenses so easily and devastate factories at Stuttgart? Why were the British and Americans already landing troops near Cannes and entering Paris? Where were the Luftwaffe, the Panzers, and the great offensive blitzkriegs of five years earlier? And why did he have to be assigned to the SS garrison reporting to the Gestapo? He hated the Gestapo.

Such sentiments were not going to ruin this last day at home. Too much idle time, he told himself. *Too much damned time*. And so, he tried ignoring this inner turmoil by concentrating on tasks—inspecting the wicker hip basket, straightening the catch net, and re-creasing the brim of his Austrian fedora for the fourth time. Everything checked-out to his satisfaction; the element of surprise clearly favored him. Nervously, he repeated his strategy, reciting it over-and-over: *Wait for the bevy to swarm, then, strike. Wait for the bevy to swarm, then, strike. . . .*

Glancing skyward, he peered south at the cloud swirling his direction. The brood swooped low upon his position. He crouched even lower. Once the bevy swarmed by, he sprang from behind the spruce leaping and slashing the air until he snared the first of the extremely rare *Lepidoptera Papilionidae*. With one hand choking the net, he unlatched the hip basket's cover and unscrewed the lid. He shook the catch into the glass jar filled with cotton swabs presoaked in ethyl acetate, the poisoning jar, and tightened the lid to observe his lone prisoner fight the effects of the fumes.

Frederick held his breath as the prey's wings froze drooping motionless. Watching the creature struggle, he sympathized over its doom. To have come this far on its journey and die so hideously could never have been imagined by the delicate butterfly, he speculated. But, soon enough, he emitted a soft shrill whistle and smiled. It had also been a long twenty-eight year wait. "Death becomes you, my friend," he whispered, "and for that I can only say I am sorry." No doubt his colleagues would be envious, he thought. No one had a collection of butterflies as grand as Professor VonObst, the foremost entomologist at University of Freiburg.

As butterflies continued to flutter by, seemingly indifferent to his presence, he regained his composure and leaped in the air for a second catch. This time he missed. He flayed again and again, leaping higher, each time failing to capture another victim.

Lili watched his attempts from the hillside near the cottage and snickered. He would scold her if he knew how amusing she found his antics. Such a child, she thought. Still, the sight of him leaping like an uncoordinated ballerina tugged at her heart. She would miss *Freddy* dearly. She would miss all his oddities including the endless fascination with insects, his excitable voice, the smell of stale pipe smoke on his mustache whenever he kissed her, and the way he slurped tea, a habit she never succeeded in refining. But she would especially miss their quiet Sunday afternoons together. She could always count on Freddy to make love to her on Sunday afternoons and sing sweetly in her ear. It was a ritual he had perfected and an act she relished. He had a way of arousing her passions and perpetuating the relentless madness to their whirlwind courtship.

From the first moment they accidentally touched, he had not been able to keep his hands off her. There was a gentleness about him unlike anyone she had ever known. That is why she surrendered so easily. When friends told her he was much too old, how students should never become involved with their professors, she refused to listen. She saw something in those eyes of his both wonderfully mischievous and irresistible. Thus, she gave into carnal temptation—the first time for her and the second time for him. And she put her graduate studies in literature and her love of poetry on hold. Even when they said he would never marry, how he would remain an eccentric bachelor, she proved them wrong—*she and the newborn.*

A soft coo distracted her thoughts and she pivoted on a picnic blanket to check their infant son. The child stirred, lifted his wobbly head and tumbled on his side, only to suck frantically on a thumb. She stroked his head, running her fingers through his wispy hair. "Hush, Jon-Jon. Go back to sleep." As if on cue, the infant closed his eyes. Such a predictable creature, she thought. Exactly like his father. Convinced the child would not reawaken, she opened her purse and took out a fountain pen and small tablet of paper. This last day with Freddy had left her melancholy and she needed to write. This is what she did when her soul stirred to a tumultuous moment—she turned to poetry. Right now, her emotions ran deep and she needed to cry. Maybe, if I scream and let it out, I'll feel better, she thought. But she possessed more composure than to succumb to screaming. Instead, she decided to channel her energy and express emotions on paper. How will I survive without my Freddy? She asked herself.

For the past year she had become so accustomed to Freddy's attentiveness, so complacent to his everyday pampering, that she had somehow grown completely dependent on her husband. These oddly insecure feelings ran counter to the once fiercely independent woman. And she never quite understood why he volunteered for this war. After all, he exceeded mandatory conscription by twenty years. Yet, in spite of repeated pleas, she failed to dissuade him. He remained adamant. "The Fatherland needs me once more," were his exact words. Hence, this conflict found her and the baby relegated to feelings of helplessness. So, sitting alone atop the hill and watching her husband leap foolishly in the meadow, she became inspired to write a new poem:

I watched you sleeping again last night,
so far away in slumber's arms,
dreaming about your field of butterflies.
And as I watched, I softly touched your face,
caressing your skin, smelling your hair,
my senses lost in you.
Then, I, too, dreamed—
dreamed of us making love,
with lovemaking so deliciously sweet,
the taste of your lips against mine

stirred my soul.
And I asked myself:
How shall I live without you by my side?
How shall I live without you?

As she pondered the answer, his cries for help interrupted her thoughts.

"Lili. Lili, come here quick. I need your help. Hurry."

She wanted to finish the stanza but her most demanding child, Freddy, wanted her, too. As always, Freddy came first. "Alright, my love. I'm coming," she whispered.

Tearing the page loose from the tablet, she folded it in fourths, placing it and the fountain pen in her blouse pocket. She raced full speed down the hill to his side. By the time she reached him, he was pulling a second catch out of the poisoning jar and needed her help to mount it.

"Look, Lili. I succeeded. To think they came all the way from Toulon to belong to me," he stated, pausing to correct himself. "I mean, *to us.*"

"I'm proud of you, Freddy. You have been amazingly patient for twenty-eight years."

"But worth the wait. Yes?"

"Yes. Well worth it."

"Lili, I need you to open my backpack. Inside is a glass shadow box with a mounting backboard. Bring them here, please."

She walked behind the spruce where the backpack had been abandoned and took out the glass box. Knowing he would want to hurriedly mount the butterflies, she slid out the stiff white backboard and returned everything to where he sat. He held the first catch by its thorax with tweezers for her to view.

"Is this butterfly not the most beautiful? So exquisite. So delicate. Look at the colors. Have you ever seen such a vibrant yellow? See how it contrasts to the black on the inner margin? Notice the tail on the hind wings, here? This is what makes them rare."

She crouched next to him, reaching in his hip basket to remove the mounting pins. She had been through the routine before but never with such a prized trophy and never with Freddy this euphoric. She rested the board on her knees facing him. He placed the body of the first butterfly in the board's groove, securing it with two pins while folding its wings flat under the twin threads running vertically the length of the board. He repeated the process, placing the second butterfly directly below the other. When he finished, she reached back to grab the frame. It was the moment when he noticed her fountain pen.

"Wait. Before we seal it I think I should sign it. Do you agree?"

She nodded. "Of course, my love. By all means."

He stole the pen and carefully scribed their names with the date in the corner of the mounting board:

Professor Frederick VonObst and wife Lili.
20 August, 1944
Schwartzwald, Germany near Freiburg
Lepidoptera Papilionidae

She grinned when he finished. "So you're giving me credit for the capture of these two noble creatures?"

"Not the capture, Lili. *The event.*" His voice rose to a shrill. "You can tell our grandchildren someday how you were there. How you witnessed it."

They slid the glass frame over the mounting board, sealing the four sides with rosin to make the box air tight. He noticed an edge had dislodged and posed a potential source for an air leak.

"This corner is warped," he fretted. "We need something to push in on the lip to seal it properly." He rummaged through the hip basket trying to find anything to serve the purpose, anything to wedge the joint tighter.

She watched his face turn frantic while searching through the basket. She listened to his groans far longer than her patience should have allowed. Such a child, she thought. Softly, she placed her hand over his and whispered, "Try this, my love." Reaching in her blouse pocket, she handed him the folded paper, pleating it once more in half. "I believe this will serve the purpose."

Without saying anything in return, he slid the wad under the wooden lip compressing the joint and, with the paper firmly wedged in place, sealed it tight with the remaining rosin.

"You always seem to know what to do, Lili. You're actually much rarer than these," he said, pointing to the entombed swallowtails. But then he noticed her eyes and the pent-up melancholy. He knew she dreaded his leaving. Today, he vowed, would be one she would never forget, melancholy or not. "Lili, why don't we climb the hill and make love? It is the most beautiful Sunday afternoon I have ever seen." He delicately grasped her hand and stood, gazing at her while encouraging her to stand. She, however, refused to budge and remained seated in tall grass.

"Shall we go to the cottage first and have our afternoon tea?" She teased, knowing full well he wanted to devour her.

"*What*?" He replied perplexed. "Not make love in broad daylight? Out in the open on the hill? Two naked sweaty bodies surrounded by Old World Swallowtails? You must really love your tea."

"I do love my tea, Freddy, but not nearly as much as making love to you on our Sunday afternoons." She paused to look at him. Butterflies swarmed around his shoulders and he posed ethereal. "Why bother climbing the hill, dear husband? It will only tire you. Save all your energy for me," she purred before yanking him to the ground. "Besides, there is a wonderful catch for you here in the meadow."

He fell next to her. She wasted little time unsnapping the buttons on her blouse in a showy burlesque display. He watched her undress, savoring the beauty of her youth, and remained thoroughly amused by her foreplay. Once she was naked, she snatched the fedora from his head and spun it to the ground. He wasted little time, sitting on his knees to embrace her and pulling her into him. And that afternoon they made love in their meadow deep in the heart of the Black Forest while millions of butterflies, rare Old World Swallowtails, danced around their bodies. Then, he sang in her ear:

Underneath the lantern, by the barrack gate,
Darling I remember the way you used to wait;
'Twas there that you whispered tenderly,
That you loved me,
You'd always be,
My Lili of the lamplight,
My own Lili Marlene . . . .

The next day, as ordered, he reported for duty at Bergen-Belsen.

(1972)

The train from Marseilles to Stuttgart should have lulled the American soldier to sleep. The rhythmic swaying from side to side, even the predictable clatter of wheels against rails should have helped him doze. God only knew he needed the rest having slept less than two hours the past three days. Nothing, however, could drown the anguish of Richard O'Malley, captain of the U.S. Army's Special Forces Red Unit. AWOL for the fifth straight day, he had become a wanted man on the run. One of West Point's most highly decorated soldiers had brazenly defied orders. Up to this incident he bore all the leadership credentials career military officers needed for promotion—courage, honor, unwavering loyalty, and a normally cool head under fire—but not today. Today, he had become a casualty of war, a lousy war—*Vietnam.*

He thought the stint in Germany would last longer. Not so. Too many buddies had been killed in action the past year. Too many lives had been lost in the Mekong Delta and the DMZ. Now his commanders needed him back in South Vietnam to lead the latest batch of green draftees who failed to dodge the war. The brass needed an experienced warrior to guide more broods through rice paddies and teach nineteen-year-olds how to kill and ambush an enemy impossible to identify. The new assignment would be his third tour to Southeast Asia. He had volunteered for the other stints but not this one. In '67 his advisory role seemed honorable; in '69 it seemed tolerable. Now, in 1972, it seemed suicidal. It had become a non-winnable war mired in politics, killing innocent people without any real objective.

And for the first time in his life he felt as if God had abandoned him and his country. This was not what he envisioned as a youth in Iowa. These were not the values his parents instilled. When he left for the Academy, the entire town bid him farewell. They hailed him a hero. He was the one mothers pointed to with pride and told their sons to emulate. Now, those sons were the draftees and he had to write the mothers how their children died bravely and honorably, and he simply could not do it any longer. But what to do next became the issue. Resign dishonorably? Hide? Do the tour anyway? It was a decision only he could make. So, he remained alone on the train, a forsaken man teetering on the abyss. And if hell existed, it had made itself a home in his tormented mind. It was why he remained sleepless and why he could not live with his conscience any longer.

He sat up straight and leaned against the coach window with his head bouncing against glass, ignoring the countryside whisking by. Like yesterday and the day before, he had yet to decide whether to report back to Stuttgart or seek shelter in Switzerland. Some of his friends fled to Geneva a week earlier. Why shouldn't he? He wondered. And if this inner debate kept him riled, the noise ten rows behind most definitely kept him angry. A group of youth had ignored courtesy signs by smoking pot and blasting Rolling Stones tunes on their tape player. He grew convinced the trio were singling him out by deliberately distracting his efforts at sleep.

"I've got to sleep. Got to sleep," he kept mumbling.

But the noise continued to tease unabated. Worse, the distracters gave him something else to focus on—anything to keep from resolving his decision.

He noticed the three hippies when they boarded in France. He hated hippies. He hated everything they stood for: immorality, laziness, pacifism, and filth—filth that came with unwashed clothes and days without bathing. Worse, they sounded like American kids, the type who disdained the industrial-military establishment he swore to uphold. He guessed they were only a few years younger and probably on their way to the big anti-war rally in Bonn. No doubt rich mommy and daddy were footing the travel bill. Anything to keep the neighbors and acquaintances at the country club from knowing the truth how little Johnny and Susie had embraced LSD and turned their backs on the material world. After all, hippies have no money—*they don't work*. How else would they have gotten there?

"Lazy hippies," he muttered. "They don't have a clue how the world works. Not a damn clue."

The more he thought about the three, the angrier he became. If not the marijuana smoke irritating his sinuses, *their God-awful music* wore thin his weary nerves. Sons of bitches need to be taught a lesson, he mulled. Impulsively, he stood and spun around; his eyes dilated and his fists clenched. The hippies had succeeded in consuming his attention and for the first time in days he did not have to focus on himself. The disciplined uniform, now soiled from days of impromptu meals on the run and nights dodging M.P.'s, bore no resemblance to its once properly starched and pressed appearance. He ignored the crumbs and other debris scattered across his lap and bolted headlong to where they sat.

Two bearded men, their scraggly shoulder-length hair matted from weeks of uncombed attention, and an attractive young woman were laughing hysterically, passing around a joint. She appeared to be a novice, coughing with each deep toke. One of the men spoke with an Arkansas drawl; the other man's obnoxious New Jersey diction caused him to cringe. The woman, however, spoke with a distinct German accent. Her long blond hair had been ironed straight. Wisps of it flowed across the shoulders of her Mexican-styled wedding blouse. She wore a peace medallion. It dangled on a delicate gold chain and looked more like a jewelry statement than a medallion—solid gold, garnished generously with diamonds and emeralds. He smirked watching her and speculated how much *Oma* and *Opa* splurged on the charm. These clearly were not ordinary hippies, he surmised. They were the worst kind—*the ones without ideals*—who only acted out the charade and faked conviction to be cool. They were the high-fashion sort living off parents' wealth waiting to inherit the keys to the financial kingdom. And right now the only thing the trio appeared to have a conviction for? *Smoking pot.* Even after a minute of scrutiny, they still failed to notice his looming six-foot four-inch frame or his swift one-handed yank on the ornate medallion, ripping it from the girl's neck. He threw the object the length of the coach until it exploded against the plate glass of an exit door. The woman looked up in horror as her bloodshot eyes strained to focus. The men did nothing to protect her, too stoned to appreciate his rage. One flashed a sheepish smile and waved a peace sign with two fingers but the soldier wasted little time on the conciliatory gesture. He cursed and grabbed the Southern-sounding man by the throat.

"*Peace*. Huh? You don't know the meaning of the damned word you little shit. How dare you question your country. How dare you challenge what's made America great. And you," he screamed at the woman, "I wouldn't expect this behavior from *your kind*. Have you no pride? No shame? If it wasn't for people like me you'd be saluting the hammer and sickle right now. To hang out with these two scum, why. . . *why, you're nothing but a goddamn whore*."

He freed the grip on the man's throat and raised a fist high in the air to backhand the woman's face. She flinched. He hesitated for a second but succumbed to his rage and swept downward. It was the unseen other hand that stopped the assault and caught the fist short of its intended target. It belonged to the conductor, an even larger man in his late thirties.

"Sir. Please, sir. Take your seat. I can't allow this sort of behavior on my train."

Richard O'Malley glared at the conductor and back at the young woman. His face contorted as the gravity of the situation set in. Striking a woman violated his code of honor and ran counter to the small town Iowa values he held dear. Allowing the three hippies to get under his skin meant his mental state had deteriorated beyond his moral code of decency. He yanked his fist from the conductor's grip. "I'm sorry," he mumbled.

"Most of us here aren't like this one," the conductor responded, pointing to the woman. "Most of us appreciate everything your country has tried to do. But we've also learned violence is not the answer."

"Yes, you're right," he replied, staring at the floor too

ashamed to look up. Embarrassed, he staggered back to his seat and collapsed, consumed by his own misbehavior.

I must be losing my mind. I would never strike a woman, he thought. Oh dear Lord, please help me. Should I keep going? Should I get off? Turn myself in or search for ghosts? He moaned aloud, rocking back and forth as his face contorted over the decision. "Gotta sleep. Need sleep. Need sleep."

An announcement over the P.A. system stirred him from the ranting. Eyeing his duffel bag, he unzipped the side compartment and began pulling out its contents one by one, tossing clothes on the floor until he found his prized possession, the glass shadow box with two butterflies. He read the inscription in the corner under glass and leaned back in his seat and stared out the window.

"Sir, the next stop is Freiburg," the conductor announced for a second time. "Will you be getting off or traveling to Stuttgart?"

Richard O'Malley peered up at the man. "I'll be getting off in Freiburg," he answered. "Yes. Freiburg it is."

(2000)

It was a shrill chirping that startled him from slumber. The sound emanated, not from the ordinary twitter one associates with birds, but from an electronic ringer of a factory preset telephone, one of the newer digital types he despised. His wife had slyly coaxed him into buying the contraption in Texas. And from the moment he first laid eyes upon it at the high-tech superstore it intimidated him. Even when he brought it back to the Colorado vacation house and attempted to set it up, he never quite understood how to change the pre-installed options. So, he never adjusted the ringer-gizmo-thingy. Now he wished he had. Now it screamed at him like a caged roadrunner and he could not stop it except to pick up the handset, something he refused to do. *"Why can't you just ting-a-ling?"* He yelled at it.

When he finished chastising the device, he yawned and wiped mucus from the corners of his eyes. His left cheek bore a red crease where the corner of his laptop supported his collapsed head. A wad of saliva pooled near the mouse pad. He wiped it off with a shirt sleeve and cringed. Whenever he drooled it meant snoring preceded. Fortunately, no one was there to complain about the 'human wind tunnel.' He was alone except for the chirping—the incessant *frigging* chirping.

Mitchell Jameson thought about yanking on the mounting cord and dislodging it once and for all, but refrained from the impulse. Maybe the caller was Susan. He glanced at the calendar, the one she made him as a Christmas gift with their photographs printed above each month. Staring at the calendar, he shook his head. Where had the year gone? The millennium began great, he remembered, but suddenly everything changed. It started with the discovery in his mother's attic. Now, stalled in self-doubts, anger consumed his emotions because of the lies. Or was it the truth? He had conveniently forgotten. Right now, the only truth chirped nonstop. He glared at the phone and reluctantly lifted the handset.

"*Hello.*"

"Mitchell, is this really you?"

"Who else would it be?"

The voice belonged to Mitchell's literary agent, Harvey

Klanowitz. "Well, buddy boy, I've been looking everywhere for you. I should have known you'd go to the mountain getaway. You've got everyone worried, especially Susan and the girls and—"

"And, obviously, my literary agent who's been hounding me for another novel," he interrupted.

"Actually, at this point we're only concerned about your wellbeing. You left Austin without telling anyone. You should have told me what was going on. Are you okay?"

"Yes."

"Susan called and told me everything. She was bawling her eyes out. You upset her."

"I know."

"You're lucky she hasn't left you. Want to talk about it?"

"*No.*"

"Have you talked to anyone about it? *Anyone professionally*?"

"Like a counselor?"

"That's what I mean."

"Yeah. Found one in the HMO book. Picked her at random. Before I left, I told Susan I'd do at least that much—seek help."

"Well, get a good one."

"Is there such a thing?"

"Sure. When Doris and I had problems, we went to a marriage counselor. We worked out issues. Hey, thirty years together ain't bad."

"No. Not bad, Harvey."

"So, how long have you two been married? Five years?"

"Seven."

"Ah-h-h, the old seven-year-itch thing." Harvey chuckled. "Well, are you going to call Susan? I know she wants to talk with you."

"I'm sure she does. I just don't want to deal with her right now. I need to focus on me. I don't feel good about myself, Harvey. That's why I came here—to get away from everyone and everything *including you.*"

"Then tell me this. Is the girlfriend there with you?"

"No. She's part of the problem. Why would I bring her here?"

"Hey. Don't kill the messenger. I'm the guy looking out for you."

"Harvey. I don't make a habit of infidelity. Not like *some people I know.* She was the first and the last. I've never played around on my wife before. Ever."

"But Susan found out. You got caught."

"Getting caught wasn't the problem. The problem was cheating in the first place. It's called breaking vows, the vows made before God. You remember your vows, don't you Harvey?"

"Of course I do but you are the asshole who cheated and got caught. Not me."

Mitchell laughed uneasily. "You're absolutely correct. Sorry. So, why did you call me? Is it because you wanted to know if I started the next book? If I'm writing again?"

"As long as you brought it up."

Mitchell sneered. "Well, *yes.* I finally started a new one."

"That's great. *Great.* Maybe this thing's got the old creativity churning. The adrenaline pumping. Maybe it's what was needed to inspire you and get—"

"Shut up, Harvey. If you think this is what I needed to start writing again, you're more messed up than me."

"No, that's not what I meant."

"Yes, it is."

"No, really. What I meant was sometimes writing can be cathartic. A way to heal. I've always told you that your books are good but lack the passion of Hemmingway or F. Scott Fitzgerald. Those guys poured, no, *splashed* feelings into their books. You could always tell what was going on in their personal lives by the tone of their books. Who knows, maybe Susan can be your *Zelda*?"

"You're clearly out of your mind."

"Hey, I just want you to run with the moment. Do you know how long it's been since you've been on the bestseller list?"

"Twenty-six months, three days."

"There. See? It's gotta be killing you. Four straight best sellers and, then, nothing."

"Yeah, I know. It just bothers me to think I had to screw around on my wife to get inspired."

"Hey, whatever it takes, my friend. So, when will you be done?"

"*When I get to the last period on the last page.*"

"Uh-huh. What's it about?"

"Harvey, it's bad luck to discuss an unfinished book. Forget it."

"That means you don't have it figured out yet, do you?"

"Of course I do. I'm superstitious. I want this one to be my best."

"Bullshit. I know you, buddy boy. If you knew the plot,

you would have already told me."

"I know the plot, Harvey. It's about two men. Two men separated in time. Who question their lives, their countries, and their moral values. They're caught in wars tearing them away from loved ones and the beliefs they hold dearest."

"So, these two guys do what? Get called off to war?"

"Yeah."

"And they have to leave their girlfriends behind?"

"Not their *girlfriends*. Their wives."

"Okay, whatever. Their *wives*. Excuse me. So, they leave their wives and go off to war and do what?"

"*Do what*? They're forced to deal with the realities of war. They have to change to survive. You know, what butterflies go through during metamorphosis."

"*Butterflies*?"

"The Butterflies of Toulon. The swallowtails in the south of France."

"I don't have a clue what you're talking about. Just whatever the hell you're doing, keep it up. It's obvious you're on a roll. And let me tell you something: the fans are clamoring for more Mitchell Jameson novels. Finish the damn book—*soon*."

"And Klanowitz Literary Agency wants results from their six figure advance. Right?"

"Yup. That's right. You're the hottest ticket in town. Get the counseling. Okay? The counseling? I'll even pay for it."

"Tomorrow, Harvey. It's set for tomorrow."

"Good. And keep working on the butterflies or whatever the hell it is—*the war stuff*."

"Real nice, Harvey. That's the last time I ever tell you

anything. The last time."

"Ha. I'll call you in a few days. I'm going to telephone Susan and let her know you're writing again. It's a good sign."

"Maybe." Mitchell shrugged. "Do me a favor. Tell Susan I won't be in Colorado forever. I'll call her in a few days. I simply need more time to myself. And tell her that I love her."

"You got it, Mitchell. *Ciao, my man.*"

Mitchell Jameson hung up the phone. He reached for the wall jack, squeezed the plug's tongue and dislodged the mounting cord. He turned back to the laptop and began writing with his imagination racing.

TWO
(1944)

The recruits stood shoulder to shoulder, chests puffed exaggeratedly, as their commandant strutted in front. The seasoned SS officer carefully scrutinized their uniforms with a monocle wedged in his puckered brow. The leader towed a host of underlings wearing the same styled ensemble—bulging-hip riding pants above high-top boots; waist-length jackets with shiny brass buttons and gold lightning bolt insignias; short-brimmed officers' hats topped with Reich eagle pennants centered in front. As anticipated, the inspection did not take long. Only five recruits stood at attention, half as many as the previous week and a third as many as the entire review team. The commandant felt fortunate to have any soldiers. The eastern front with Russia had extracted a heavy toll on Germany's ability to supply his compound. His best combat-ready guards had been pulled away months earlier and replaced with the likes of these five. He cringed parading by the newcomers. Stopping in front of each, he repeatedly corrected posture, repositioned sidearms, re-tilted caps. Given the state of Germany's readiness to defend the homeland, these were token replacements incapable of managing the swelled prisoner population. Worse, barely enough bullets remained to stop an insurrection where his forces would be outnumbered a hundred to one. The predicament both worried and angered him. These five recruits were anything but soldiers. They were children and old men donning polished boots and swastikas playing a grownup game. All five would soon be robbed of innocence.

Three of the recruits were under the age of seventeen. One appeared in his early fifties. And the last one in line appeared to be in his mid-seventies and quite ancient.

"Welcome to Bergen-Belsen, Stalag 4. My name is Heinrich Goerne, *Commandant* Heinrich Goerne." He paused to study their faces. Misfits, he thought. Total misfits. He cleared his throat with a hack. "Let there be no misunderstanding, *gentlemen,* who I am, what I am. *I am God.* Your God. Our prisoners' God. I rule this post controlling both life and death. Never question my absolute authority—my power to give and take life. My superiors with the Gestapo in Berlin certainly don't. They do not interfere with my work here and I do not question their work there. They supply me prisoners and I supply them war goods. Never question my tactics. Submit yourself freely and unconditionally and we will get along splendidly. Do not and you will regret it. Do you understand?" He barked.

Silence prevailed. The recruits' eyes focused straight ahead. It pleased him. It encouraged him. Perhaps, this batch could be molded into well-trained warriors and, soon, be trusted inside Section A.

"Like you, before the war I was a civilian. A doctor by trade in a long ago life. A different life. With the war I surrendered my past and have since learned to embrace today's reality. You will too. You will change or perish. In war only the most determined survive. The choice is all yours. Once you have proven your ability to adapt to the conditions here, once you have proven your loyalty to me and to the Führer, you will be called upon. Do not fail to heed the call for failure is not acceptable. Those who fail rob Germany of her rightful place in history."

As he spoke eyeing them, he slapped the palm of a gloved hand with a leather riding crop. The crisp impacts startled the three youngest recruits.

"You have been chosen to help manage the oldest of the Führer's detention factories. This factory is essential for the continuation of our war effort. We produce supplies for our fighting men on the battlefields. The smoke stacks bear witness to our twenty-four hour efforts. Your responsibility will be to feed the workers, thus insuring they remain healthy and able to meet our quotas. Quotas are necessary to sustain our troops. *We must meet our quotas*.

"You will also notice how we have been spared the bombings of neighboring factories. It is because this post is considered a prisoner of war camp, protected from such atrocities by the Geneva Convention. Notice behind me is a series of three barbed wire fences. These are designed to contain our workers. Most of them are political prisoners, enemies of the State of Germany. Have no sympathy for them. They have defiled our country. They threaten our very ability to win this war and they must be contained. We have never had a prisoner escape. Should one escape, our status as a POW camp could be jeopardized. If one gets beyond Section B and the last tier of fencing, shoot to kill. Are there any questions?"

Again, only silence. It pleased him. He looked at the eldest recruit. "Which of you is Stefan Litz?"

"I am, sir," the old one replied, his shoulders stiffening.

Heinrich smiled. "Of course you are. Of course. So, according to your papers you did not serve in the last war but now you have decided to assist us here. *Why?*"

"Because Germany needs me, Sir. I love my country. I was too old to fight in the last war but not this time. This time I am younger in heart and younger in mind. And it may be my last chance to make a difference, sir."

"I see." Heinrich chuckled, mocking the man. "And where is it you discovered this fountain of youth which makes you young enough to fight after twenty-eight years? That makes you now invincible?"

"Up here, sir," Stefan responded, pointing to his head. "I realized I am only as old as I feel young. Right now I feel very young, sir. I feel invigorated by the opportunity to serve and to serve under you."

"And how will you feel after eighteen straight hours of peeling potatoes? How will that *head* of yours feel then?" The commandant gritted, jabbing the old man in the temple with the riding crop.

Stefan winced in pain before replying straight-faced, "Like a potato head, sir."

The three youngest recruits laughed, falling from ranks. The commandant snapped at each of them. "Get back in line you imbeciles. Attention. Attention."

Frederick VonObst laughed, too. He had experienced officers like Heinrich in the previous war; he knew Heinrich's type all too well. He remembered how firing squads became their instruments of obedience. He spoke out. "*Sir*. Excuse me, sir. If I may be so bold as to make a suggestion?"

"And you must be Corporal VonObst?"

"Yes, sir."

"Well, what is it Corporal?"

"Sir, it is evident these men have not experienced the true

rigors of war or learned to appreciate the importance of discipline. They aren't *like our kind*. Their individuality needs to be beaten and stripped, so they can learn to follow orders. If you will allow me to become their leader, I am sure I can whip them into shape in no time. When I am done, they will do anything you ask without question."

"Ah-h-h-h, good suggestion. Well-spoken <u>Sergeant</u>."

"*Sergeant?*"

"Yes, Sergeant. I saw your war record. Quite impressive. You must have fought next to my uncle at the Argonne Forest. Do well molding this group and I will give you more boys and old men to lead. Agreed?"

"Yes, sir."

The commandant did an about-face and marched back to his headquarters inside the secretive confines of Section A. The well-dressed entourage followed. One lieutenant remained behind, a man no more than twenty. He ordered Sergeant VonObst and the small band of volunteers to their barrack in Section B. When he departed their company, Frederick cautioned Stefan. "You need to be careful, my old friend. I have dealt with our commandant's type before. They can either be your best friend or your worst enemy. Right now we need only best friends. Understand?"

"Yes, you are right," Stefan responded, his eyes lighting with curiosity. "And what name do you go by Sergeant?"

"Freddy. But around the officers always address me formally."

"Freddy, huh?" The old one chuckled. "It sounds like a pet's name. I assume Freddy is the name your wife has given you. Yeah?"

"Yes."

"And do we have a snapshot of her to share with us lowly privates?" Stefan teased, looking at the three young men next to him for support.

"Of course," Frederick replied, pulling out his wallet, flashing the latest photo and permitting everyone to marvel at the beauty of his wife.

"She is a goddess—*a trophy*. Much younger. Yeah?"

"Yes."

The boys made obscene gestures. Frederick snatched the snapshot back and scolded them. "Crudeness will not be tolerated. Give me fifty pushups. That's an order."

The three dropped to the floor, grumbling all the while, but obeyed him, nevertheless. Frederick stood over each barking in their ears. Even with a full verbal barrage, they were not overly intimidated. How could anyone with a pet name of *Freddy* be bad or cruel? He appeared more a father-figure than a Nazi superior. Stefan looked on, amused by their efforts. The three boys collapsed after twenty pushups.

"And what about you?" Frederick blurted. "I think you should join them *now*."

"No, no, no," Stefan replied, wagging his finger. "Look at me, Freddy. I cannot do pushups. Why, if I get on the floor, I will throw out my back. Then, you and the others will have to pick me up, stand me in a hot shower and wait days for me to heal. Meanwhile, you will have to peel my share of the potatoes while I lay sprawled in my bunk and—"

"*Enough, Stefan.*" Frederick cut him off, frustrated by the childlike irreverence. "I am beginning to understand you better by the minute. Just see if you can keep out of trouble. *Okay?*"

"Okay." Stefan shrugged his shoulders. "By the way, since we will be cooking for the post, would you enjoy a good bratwurst sandwich? I make the best bratwurst sandwiches in the world. Perhaps, we can borrow some kitchen supplies and I can show you how it is done. Everyone raves about my bratwurst. *Everyone.* I use only the best ingredients, you know—the finest Danish provolone, lettuce from northern Italy, sauerkraut from Bremen, mustard from Dijon."

The rest of the day the younger troops drilled in the art of warfare beginning with how to peel five thousand potatoes in less than eighteen hours. Stefan chattered nonstop, mostly telling stories, and Frederick already missed Lili, questioning for the second time his impetuous decision to run off to war.

(1972)

When the express train stopped in Freiburg, Captain Richard O'Malley stepped onto the station platform, duffel bag in hand, not sure which direction to go or exactly where to begin. Ready to embark on his journey, a familiar sound disrupted his thoughts. Muffled between the drone of the train's idling diesel engine and P.A. announcements, he detected a staccato of frantic wheezes, as if someone was drowning and gasping at last breaths before re-submerging. It was the same sound his mother made during an asthma attack. Alarmed, he spun around. The young German woman he had accosted earlier bent hunched over, desperately gulping air. She must have stepped off the train, he guessed, to escape the stagnant confines of the coach car. The smoke must have irritated her lungs.

"Are you okay?" He asked, placing his hand on her shoulder.

Carefully measuring her breaths, she attempted to stand erect and answer him but she remained far too frazzled to respond and appeared embarrassed by the commotion she caused. Eventually, she regained enough composure to wipe the corners of her mouth; her hands trembled as she patted her lips. Her eyelids had nearly swollen shut, sandwiched with tears cascading onto her Mexican wedding blouse. "I'll be fine. I'm an asthmatic. Smoke constricts my lungs." She licked her lips to replace moisture stolen moments earlier and paused to look into his eyes. There was something different about him, she sensed—a softness not noticed before. "I must be m-m-making a spectacle out here," she stammered.

"Doesn't matter," he said. "What matters is you're breathing." He pulled out a handkerchief and wiped phlegm off her blouse while studying her gaunt face. Her skin had turned ashen; her arms raised heavy with goose bumps. She must have deliberately avoided sunlight for months, he thought. She could have easily passed as an albino. Oddly, her cheeks glowed red, highlighting the blue of her eyes and the exquisite wide cheekbones often seen in old world Bavaria. It was her eyes that drew him in. She was beautiful but frail and gossamer as a butterfly. And as he studied her appearance, he was reminded of the earlier confrontation in the coach car and he became ashamed. How could he have not noticed the innocent beauty of this delicate creature? "Look, what went on inside there, on the train. I'm sorry. Very sorry. I haven't slept in days. I've been going through some personal problems but don't honestly have an excuse for my behavior. I'm not always an ass."

"I believe you," she responded flat out.

"*You do?*"

"Yes."

"Oh? I just figured my type was considered the enemy or something."

"I don't have any enemies. Hatred is something I don't have time for. Life is too short for hatred. As far as your *type*, you're actually more a hero to me than an enemy."

"I assumed since you were with those two creeps that—"

"Captain. You are a captain, right?"

"Yes."

"Never *assume*, Captain. Looks can be deceiving. I am traveling with those two boys because we are classmates at U.C. Berkeley. This is my summer vacation and they came home to stay with my family in Frankfurt and tour Europe and see the world and—" She stopped mid-sentence. It suddenly occurred to her the two of them were alone on the station platform, Freiburg being but a remote hamlet in rural Bavaria. "And why are you disembarking here in Freiburg? There are no U.S. bases here."

"I have personal business to attend to."

"*Here*? How strange. I hope you speak German. This is the most conservative corner of my country. They pride themselves on *not* speaking foreign tongues, especially Americanized English."

He removed his hat and twirled it nervously. His journey suddenly seemed weightier. "Fact of the matter, Ma'am, I don't speak German at all. The only German words I know probably shouldn't be repeated around a lady."

"Well, what are you going to do? How are you going to get around?"

"I'll figure out something. I'm a pretty resourceful guy."

She fretted, biting her lip and shaking her head, wrestling with a decision. She motioned for him not move. She scrambled to the train's staircase and disappeared, only to return a moment later with her backpack slung over a shoulder.

"Let's go," she said.

"Wait a minute," he countered. "Us? Go? You can't leave. What about those two boys inside? You don't want to leave them, do you? Heck, I'm not even sure where I'm heading."

"They know their way to Frankfurt. They will be fine. You are the one I am worried about. As for me, I will catch the train tomorrow. Besides, I know my way around Freiburg. My parents have a summer cottage here, less than a kilometer away. It borders the Black Forest. I used to come here all the time in the summers."

"But I feel lousy imposing on you."

"Well, you are." She winked. "Let's consider this my good deed for the day. My way of showing you that *my kind* is appreciative of Americans and that I am not a *goddamn whore*."

"You're making me feel bad." He pouted.

"Good." She smiled. "At least you have a conscience. I like that in a man. So, do you want to clue me in on where it is you need to go?"

"Well, if there's a German veteran's war office in town, I'd like to check their records. I want to find someone."

"Hm-m-m. This all sounds very mysterious, Captain. By the way, my name is Hilda Zoeybler. My friends call me Zoey."

She held out her hand. He shook it, breaking a stiff but

courteous smile.

"Pleased to meet you, Zoey. I'm Richard O'Malley. You don't want to know what my friends call me. Just call me Richard and I'll understand it means me."

As they walked from the station, the train whistle emitted two short blasts announcing its departure. He thumbed the air behind. "Zoey, it's still not too late to abandon this wreck of a human being you've hooked up with."

"Nonsense. You cannot be any worse than the two boys back there. Besides, I like projects."

He grimaced, not sure if he wanted to be lumped in with the two hippies or what she exactly meant by the remark, but this time he kept his mouth shut.

After reaching the town square, they had no trouble finding the agency responsible for German veterans. Zoey's ability to translate proved indispensable. They were able to roam freely in the library archives containing war records. He climbed the ladder, hauling down massive ledgers until the right one, the cross-referenced one inscribed "Freiburg SS Enlists, May, 1944—April, 1945," was located. The weighty book indexed alphabetically. He flipped through pages until he found the name 'Frederick VonObst.'

"So, this is who you are trying to locate," she whispered.

"Yes, but most of his war information has been erased. It's as if someone purposely removed it."

Zoey reviewed what little information was available. "You are right, Richard. There is not much here. All it says is he volunteered in August, 1944, and served honorably at Bergen-Belsen for nine months, got promoted immediately to the rank of sergeant, and was released from duty in May, 1945.

It says he died in 1949, but does not say how. It does not say if he has any survivors but does indicate he was married. There is no status on his wife or a forwarding address. According to the notation, he was buried outside of town at the veteran's cemetery."

"That's it?"

"Yes, I am sorry."

He stared at the ceiling, frustrated by the inability to uncover anything noteworthy. The dream-like apparitions of his childhood memories would continue to haunt him unabated. However vague, the apparitions seemed destined to plague him forever.

"Are you hungry?" He finally asked.

"Thirsty and famished."

"In that case, let me take you out to dinner. It's the least I can do for all your help."

"Why, thank you. I would like dinner with you. There is a café around the corner. No one will recognize you there."

"Why would you say that?"

"Because it's apparent you are man on the run. U.S. Army officers don't wear wrinkled and stained uniforms."

"It's that obvious?"

She grabbed his hand and led him out the door. "It is only obvious to someone who notices small things, like the exhaustion on your face."

"I guess I'm more of a mess than I thought."

"Troubled, perhaps. Mess, no. Look, you can tell me what is going on over a tall stout. Yes?"

A relaxing beer sounded fine to him and, as promised, she found her small restaurant. It served pizza and beer, a rarity for the pro-ethnic German region. They ordered two large "Bismarck Specials" with pepperoni and extra cheese. By the second beer, he became more willing to reveal his secrets. During the course of their conversation he watched her down an assortment of pills.

"What are those for?" He pried.

"These are supposed to help me control my asthma. One is a dehydrator. One is a mild suppressant. One contains some sort of steroid, and the other . . . I forgot." She laughed. "I am supposed to take them twice a day with plenty of liquid. I would say two beers qualify for plenty of liquid."

"Absolutely."

He raised his stein. She clanked hers against his before curiosity coaxed her to a next question.

"So, do you want to tell me why you are really here?"

With the question, he couldn't help but focus on her eyes again. There was something familiar about them—something triggering his memories. She struck him as an old soul from a past life. Instinct told him she could be trusted. And he needed someone to listen to his woes and believe in his worth both as a man and a soldier. Only hours earlier he had lost all hope. Now, she was there as if sent from heaven in the nick of time to rescue him. Why not? He told himself. *Why not*? "I'm on the run, Zoey. I'm AWOL. I'm in hiding from the military police. I was supposed to report to Stuttgart five days ago to take command of a company of Rangers. We were relieving a group in Vietnam. It was going to be my third tour in Southeast Asia. This one wasn't voluntary—it was ordered. I've got real objectionable concerns returning to war, the way it's being fought, the way we're needlessly killing our young men. So,

I've been traveling and deciding what to do. As of today, I haven't made up my mind. I guess I could always report to Stuttgart. I'd get my ass reamed once I got back but I figure the worst they could do is boot me out. More than likely, they'd sentence me to Vietnam. Or—"

"*Or?*"

"Or I could lay low for a while until I decide what to do. I've thought about seeking amnesty in Switzerland. Problem is once you apply for amnesty, you have to renounce U.S. citizenship. I'm not ready to renounce America."

"But I take it that is not the reason you got off the train in Freiburg?"

"No, that's not why. You see, my wife. . . . my wife left me last week. She took our son and went back to the states. She's already filed for divorce. When she found out I was going overseas on my third tour, she said she couldn't take being an Army widow anymore. I guess I've been too much the absentee husband. A father in photographs only. It's the nature of my job. It takes me away for long stretches. We both knew the situation when we married. We both knew there'd have to be sacrifices made. Suddenly, my lifestyle isn't acceptable. That part hurts. She always knew the military was my calling. What I prepared my life for. I love the military—hate *Vietnam*." He winced with the word. "You know, I can't imagine being a civilian again. Wow, what a change. People like me drown in a world without wars. We're not good for much else."

"I am very sorry, Richard. It all sounds horrible. There is way too much pressure on you at one time." She paused to frame her next question." Have you two been married long?"

"Almost seven years. We got hitched right out of the

Academy. Our son had his first birthday last week. Care to see his picture?"

Before she could respond, he had already reached for his billfold and unfolded a series of photos chronologically arranged in a continuous sleeve. Seven pictures of his son dangled inches from her face. Only one picture of his wife survived.

"He resembles his father. A *real brute*," Zoey teased.

"Guess he is. Scares the hell out of the cat. . . . "

She watched his face rejoice talking about his boy. "That looks good on you, Richard."

"What?"

"Your smile. It is the first time today you have broken a scowl. You had better be careful. We don't want to overdo it. You might pass out."

"You're teasing me again, aren't you?"

"Of course I am. Such a straight-laced military man. Give me a week and I will have you smiling every day."

"I believe you could, Zoey. I believe you could."

They talked the rest of the afternoon but later he became anxious to visit the grave site of Frederick VonObst. He paid the bill. They walked to the edge of town and onward to the cemetery for German war dead. No one was there to assist them in the search. She started at one end and he the other. When they finally stumbled upon the correct plot, the sun peered low on the horizon. August evenings tend to cool quickly in the Black Forest region. She shivered. He took his jacket off and draped it over her shoulders; it hung to her knees. She sensed he wanted solitude and stepped back giving him privacy. She still had no idea what role Frederick VonObst played in his life or the purpose behind the long awaited reunion.

Staring at the headstone, Richard O'Malley said nothing. He eventually knelt and brushed debris from the marker where it could be more easily read. No flowers or other signs of remembrances were visible like the other gravesites. This one had not been visited for some time. The marking simply bore Frederick VonObst's name and the dates, 1892—1949. He solemnly touched the headstone with the flat of his palm but abruptly stood up.

"What? No ceremony? No prayer?" Zoey inquired.

"Not today. I'm too tired. I need to sleep."

"But, *Hansel*," she baited, "you know I am a curious *Gretel*. I must know what this man means to you and why you are really here. You avoided my earlier interrogation." She smiled.

He turned to look in her eyes. He knew she wouldn't stop until he answered all her questions. He could also tell she was concerned, genuinely concerned. And he decided to share the secret.

"Okay, Zoey. You win. I think this man is my father."

"*Your father*. But, but how could—"

He placed his finger over her lips. There would be no more revelations this day. He had succeeded in his long standing search for answers. Now he was tired and needed to sleep.

"Tomorrow, *Gretel*," he yawned, his arms stretching high in the air. "We'll talk more tomorrow. Now, are there any quiet hotels in Freiburg with nice cozy beds?"

"I don't know much about hotels but there is always my parent's cottage. *And it is free*."

"Wouldn't they object to their daughter housing a

deserter?"

"Don't be silly. They trust my judgment. Come. It is only a short walk from here. Come."

They followed a winding road out of Freiburg leading to where the Black Forest began and to a cottage on a hill tucked next to a vast meadow. And there, he found solace for the first time in days with his long-standing turmoil drowned in much needed slumber.

(2000)

Mitchell should have recognized something amiss. He should have known from the outset, especially given the multitude of inferred signals—the receptionist with the crewcut casting dirty looks his direction, the waiting room magazines broadcasting gay and lesbian lifestyles, the female couple holding hands. He should have also paid attention to the obvious—the sign hanging outside: "Counseling for Alternative Living." But he failed to notice anything unusual. Why should he? He had been preoccupied by the events of the previous day and too engrossed in writing the likes of which he had not done in years. Hence, when the counselor invited him into her office and guffawed as if she had just heard a good joke, he, naturally, didn't notice. After all, it was his first encounter with a bona fide psychologist, a profession of which he knew little. He was only there because he promised Susan and Harvey he would attempt to seek help. Only half-committed to the exercise, he had to at least go through the motions.

"You must be Mitchell. I'm Dr. Laura Blumenthal."

"Pleased to meet you—*I think.*"

"I detect hesitancy. No problem. Since you indicated you've never been through counseling before, I can appreciate the apprehension. Believe it or not, some people learn to actually look forward to it. 'Sort of gives them a chance to talk nonstop about themselves. Forces someone else to listen."

"Uh-huh."

"I take it you've had a chance to look over our fees? You're on a HMO. After today, your hour-long sessions will only cost your friend, Mr. Klanowitz, $25 each. Not bad. I've seen worse."

"Uh-huh."

"I'll also assume you've read our statement of policy, our philosophy here?"

"Huh-Huh?"

"No? Hm-m-m-m. Well, Mitchell, almost all my work is spent exclusively helping lesbian couples sort out their problems. Maintaining a healthy relationship in today's topsy-turvy world with a partner has always been a challenge. But my special area of interest is helping the modern gay family cope with the stresses of life. You know, problems that tend to tear at a couple's moral fabric. Oh, and by the way, I am a lesbian as is my entire staff. Does my admission shock you?"

His mouth fell open. "Uh-huh."

"Well, why?"

He hesitated before responding, realizing the question had forced him to utter more than two syllables. "I'm not sure," he responded tactfully.

"Are you unsure of my qualifications? Or unsure if I can

help you?"

"Not sure if you can relate to me."

"Well, I don't have a penis, if that's what you mean, although I have fantasized about growing one." She giggled. "But my sexual orientation should not affect anything unless you allow it to," she replied, drawing a puzzled look. "And how did you locate me, anyway?"

"At random. Closed my eyes. Ran my finger down a list and presto—your name."

"Uh-huh."

"Look, Doctor, I don't care what your alternative lifestyle is. I just need a little guidance. You deal in fixing relationships. Good. Mine needs fixing. You're a woman. I'll be darned, my wife's a woman. You're probably pissed off at men. I'll be darned, my wife's pissed off at her man. All things in common. And if you can help me, I promise to never forward email jokes about gays again. Deal?"

"Hm-m-m-m, patient harbors deep-rooted hostility for alternative lifestyles," she mumbled, scratching notes in her journal. "Keep on babbling Mitchell. You're off to a good start."

"Okay, try this one on for size: Why is it most of you psychologists seem to need more help than the patients on the other side of your desks?"

"Simple," she answered, straight-faced. "It's because we have to listen to people like you all day."

"That's messed up, isn't it?"

"It's a living."

He chuckled.

"Look. Why are you here, Mitchell? Isn't it an expensive

proposition just to trade snide comments with me?"

"Not really. I find it refreshing. Besides, doesn't cost me anything. My agent's paying the tab."

"Agent? Mr. Klanowitz? Well, which are you? An actor or a writer."

"I'm an acting writer."

"Okay. When was the last time you wrote something prolific?"

"Boy, what a loaded question. I guess it's been over two years."

"Two years? Does it mean you're now in a dry spell?"

"Yeah, but I started writing again a few days ago."

"And how's it going? Are the ideas flowing?"

"Like shit through a goose."

"And does that mean it's going well or you just have *crappie ideas*?" She chuckled, amused by her own humor.

"That's a good one, Laura. You don't mind if I call you Laura, do you?"

"No. That's fine. And what should I call you?"

Mitchel thought for a few seconds. "*Mr. Fuck-up* will do nicely."

"Okay. And what did you do to deserve the title?"

"I screwed around on my wife."

"*Again*. You mean screwed around <u>again</u>?"

"No. The one and only time I've *ever* screwed around. Seven years faithful to the same woman. A few months ago I hooked up with this other woman while doing a book tour."

"Are you still seeing her?"

"Geez, why does everyone ask me that? No. I've cooled the relationship until I resolve my own problems. It's why I'm here."

"Problems? So, you admit you have problems."

"Yeah. I figure I won't be good in any relationship until I get my head on straight. And I'm feeling awfully guilty lately."

"Makes sense. Beats running around with a hard-on all day, letting the little head think for the big head. I like that approach. It tells me you're allowing logic and reason to hold sway over emotion. It tells me you're taking responsibility and might even have a conscience."

"Whatever."

"You know, Mr. Fuck-up, guilt can be a good thing, but you can't let it overpower you. Sometimes guilt can be destructive. Sometimes you can beat yourself up too much. When that happens, it clouds the real issues. It becomes a force by itself to be reckoned with. Like all things in life, you have to strike a balance. Guilt is no different. Let's try to keep it held at bay. Okay? And how long has it been since you slept with the bimbo?"

"Wow. I see you have a real command of the English language. Two weeks."

"Any reason why you suddenly jumped her? Why after seven years you let the little head dominate the big head?"

"Nothing comes to mind."

"Well, were you angry with your wife or are you just naturally horny?"

"Neither. I mean, sure, there are lots of things I don't like and am never going to change about my wife. I'm sure there's plenty she wants to change about me. All married couples have their likes and dislikes. The type of things that make them angry. Maybe even crazy. But this other woman just got to me.

She was insatiable."

"Barf. I think I'm going to throw up. What was so special about her? Her ass? Her tits? *What*?"

"Wow, you are crude. But I know what you're trying to do. You're trying to shock me back to reality. You're pulling a Howard Stern on my psyche, aren't you?"

"Or, perhaps, I want you to figure out if it was really the other woman who enticed you, if it was your wife who drove you away, or if it was something else. Something else that's been festering deep inside you for years. Or maybe," she looked at the ceiling deep in thought, "maybe, it's something that happened a few months ago. Something that made you snap." She snapped her fingers together and slid from behind her desk, her eyes wild with excitement.

He watched her sit directly in front of him on her desk. She crossed her legs. They were unshaven and exposed with no stockings. He cringed. Yet in spite of the outward proclamations for defiant feminism, he found her handsome. He guessed she was older, probably in her late thirties. She was obviously athletic. Her calves were built like a long distance runner's—*a hairy long distance runner*.

She noticed him staring at her legs and waved him back to attention. "Hello. Up here," she said, pointing to her face." As I was saying, you're an attractive man, Mr. Fuck-up. You're witty and clever. You seem to have a healthy libido. Maybe, too healthy." She frowned, tugging on her skirt. "My guess is whatever you've done in life, you've been successful. Success brings money, money brings power, power brings admirers. In short, you're the kind of man women might be attracted to. Certainly this woman wasn't your first opportunity to stray but for some reason you chose to make that leap, not simply for sex but to be romantically involved. And I don't think it was because what you leaped to was necessarily wonderful or magical. I mean, since when have husband-stealing sluts been magical? Deadly to marriages—yes. Magical—no.

"I'm guessing you're not the first married man she's been involved with. She's undoubtedly a home-wrecker. She's probably sinking her claws into someone else right now because you pushed her away. Now think about it. What virtuous values can any woman have who deliberately gets involved with a married man? Can you ever trust her in a permanent fidelis relationship? Now, reverse that thinking. How do you think your wife feels being cheated on? Hey, you broke your marriage vows. Aren't vows important to you? How do you think she feels about you right now? Will she ever trust you again?" She looked into his eyes for any hint of remorse. "Let me ask you something: Is your wife willing to take you back?"

"I think so."

"Is she willing to go to counseling with you?"

"Yes."

"Do you love her and want to make the marriage work?"

He paused as his eyes began to tear up. "Yes, very much."

"Then, let's work toward that objective. The other woman—she's history. I don't want to know the bitch's name. I never want to hear you mention her. You're going to forget the bitch starting today, cold-turkey. Do you understand?"

"Yes."

"Do I have your word on that?"

"Yes."

"Good. I want to see you twice a week starting next Tuesday. Also, next time I want you to bring me ten reasons why you love your wife. What's her name?"

"Susan."

"Fine. Next Tuesday you bring me a list of ten reasons why you married Susan in the first place and why you still love her. I'll tell you right now, if you want your marriage to work, it won't be easy. It never is but we'll get there. I promise. Now go back to your mountain chalet or wherever it is you're staying and keep plugging away at that next great American novel. Try to keep your mind occupied."

He stood and moved toward the door. She grabbed his hand, keeping him from leaving.

"One more thing," she added. "Since you've made a commitment today, you're no longer *Mr. Fuck-up*. When you walk through my door next time, you're just plain old 'Mitchell.' Is it a deal?"

"Deal." He said, shaking her hand.

THREE
(1945)

It only took Frederick VonObst three weeks to whip his small band of soldiers into shape. The same motivational techniques used on students in Freiburg also worked on "his boys"—challenge, praise, and reward (with heavy emphasis on *reward*). During the day he taught them to work as a team, both in the mess hall and on the marching field where he drilled them to the brink of exhaustion. In the evening no free time was permitted. Instead, he led them as a group in song, the soon-to-be-famous Boys Choir of Stalag 4. There were countless occasions late at night when their voices could be heard raised in unison singing German ballads, the most requested being *Lili Marlene*.

Frederick never resorted to the cruel physical abuse the SS had been known to inflict on conscripts. For that reason his small squad revered him. Soon, they began behaving like the well-disciplined soldiers he promised he would deliver to Heinrich. As a personal reward, more recruits fell under his command as they dribbled to the post in succeeding weeks. By mid-April, he commanded twenty boy-soldiers, all under the age of seventeen, with the same results as the original three. And they would do anything for him. Stefan, on the other hand, became a different story; the old man had grown beyond punishment as a motivator. From time to time Stefan simply required a kick in the rear. Still, the old man provided an essential ingredient in Frederick's reward program—the bratwurst sandwiches, a late night dividend for a hard day's work.

Months of confinement to the kitchen detail taught the squad the art of surviving war. Paramount to any such effort, however, was cultivating personal gain black-market style. Hoarding food supplies and using proceeds as barter with neighboring camps nicely served their efforts. Potatoes exchanged for eggs, eggs for butter and milk, and butter and milk for wine and schnapps.

Their skill at bartering even impressed their normally stoic commandant. Heinrich took a special liking to Frederick, especially once he discovered a doctor of entomology lay beneath the shrewd military veneer. The commandant, it turned out, had always been an avid butterfly collector himself. Thus, on numerous evenings, Frederick was invited to the private living quarters inside Section A, usually for games of chess. Bartered schnapps helped take the edge off the commandant's arrogance. Heinrich never questioned the source of the liquor or the loyalty of his most admired sergeant. During one of the nightly chess competitions, Heinrich drank a little too much and spoke too freely.

"What will you do after the war, Frederick?"

"Teach. And you?"

"I hope to retire on a military pension but, if things do not work out, I will re-open my clinic in Berlin."

"I wonder how much longer we will have before this place closes, hey, Heinrich?"

"How much longer? Until Germany is victorious, of course. However long it takes."

"But you have heard the rumors. We are being squeezed from all sides. Certainly the end is near."

Heinrich said nothing at first. He refused to dwell on such prospects, yet he trusted Frederick and the alcohol had a way of loosening his tongue. "I fear you may be right, Frederick. What do you suppose will happen to us if the truth is ever discovered about the factory?"

"The truth about the factory? Whatever do you mean?"

"You don't really know, do you?" Heinrich asked, somewhat astonished.

"I only know what you told us the first day we arrived. Don't forget, I have never been permitted *behind the fence* in Section A. I have only been permitted here, to your quarters. What could there possibly be for me to know?"

"The truth. *The ugly truth*," Heinrich whispered, gritting his teeth. "Have you never seen our prisoners?"

"Only from a distance."

"Have you never wondered why there are so many children? Why they are all emaciated? Have you never asked yourself how fifty thousand inmates can survive on five thousand potatoes and beets a day? Don't these thoughts ever cross your mind?"

Frederick glanced away without responding. He never enjoyed contemplating such things but fifty thousand inmates? *Fifty thousand*? He had no idea that many souls existed in Section A. He knew in recent weeks more and more were being shipped in by train as the Allies threatened to overrun camps closer to the border. He knew before his arrival nothing but Russian POWs made up the prisoner population, but they had been mysteriously shipped out and replaced by others. Now, the detainees comprised of dissidents, political anarchists, and traitors. He turned, returning Heinrich's glare. "No. Why should such things ever cross my mind? It is not my place to question you or the Führer. We hear rumors all the time but as far as I am concerned, they are only that—*rumors*."

Heinrich shook his head in disbelief, laughing cruelly. "You are a good obedient soldier but a lousy liar, my friend. Truth is you cannot hide what you are. You are a scientist. Your profession as an entomologist makes you naturally inquisitive. Such is your temperament. People as well-educated as us don't gain intelligence by *not* asking questions. We cannot help but ask." He paused downing the last swallow of schnapps. "Answer this for me and be truthful: How long do you think you can avoid paying attention to such things? How long can you merely look the other way to the obvious?"

"Until my conscience breaks, Heinrich."

"And when that happens?"

"When that happens, I am afraid we will not be drinking schnapps together."

Heinrich drew a deep breath and stared through his empty glass. He expected as much from his chess partner. The words saddened him, nonetheless. Men like him had few real friends. Why would Frederick be any different? And he knew he could not reveal the truth, this so-called *ugly truth*, to Frederick without jeopardizing their relationship. After all, he was a commanding officer in the elite SS. He had to concern himself with rank and orders, especially top-secret directives from the Gestapo. Lately, the dispatches had become more demanding. He could be shot for revealing such things to someone without a security clearance. He knew what the orders stipulated—a frenzied procession to the chambers. Millions of Jews had been hidden away for years, shielded from the outside world in camps all over Germany and Eastern Europe. Now they were being shipped here for one final pyre. Now there were fifty thousand wagging tongues left and a hundred thousand index fingers that could incriminate him. The inmates, *the workers*, were evidence needing to be destroyed and the process had already begun. The smoke stacks were telltale signs of the rush to death.

Heinrich finally exhaled, knowing someday soon he would have to call upon his friend to do the unthinkable. Time was running out. Looking at his friend's innocent but suspicious eyes, he raised his empty glass. "Here is to unquestioned loyalties, my friend."

Frederick reciprocated the gesture, clanking his glass against the glass of the notorious commandant of Bergen-Belsen, the man known by the inmates as *Doctor Death*.

The next day Frederick and his company of soldiers were given a one day furlough for the generous gifts presented to Heinrich. The nearby town lay in ruins from the aerial bombing raids. Bremen, less than twenty kilometers away, was no better off. Stefan suggested they spend the splendid spring day at a neighboring lake. He would pack bratwurst sandwiches for lunch. The boys could fish and swim and take their minds off the deteriorating war situation. Frederick thought it a good suggestion, although he preferred to see Lili. It had been nearly ten months since he kissed her and they had made love. A one day furlough would not provide enough time for a conjugal visit. Besides, the rail line to Freiburg had been destroyed weeks earlier by the approaching American army.

Before the group left the compound, Sergeant VonObst

lined up his squad two abreast. Stefan took the rear flank while *Freddy* meticulously inspected their uniforms. Every soldier passed with flying colors. He led them in a parade through camp, goose-stepping out the front gate as their right arms stretched to salute their commandant in a showy display of respect. Heinrich watched the procession from afar, amazed by his friend's uncanny ability to maintain such discipline. He saluted the squad and wished them a safe return.

Once the group rounded the bend, the precision-tuned soldiers quickly reverted to adolescents, a metamorphosis completed in the time it took Frederick to blow two short blasts on his whistle. The boys immediately fell out of formation, unbuttoned their stiff collars, and began the pushing and shoving matches which would characterize the rest of the day. They were a playful exuberant lot, especially enthralled to tease their leader, *Sergeant Freddy*. It was an odd dichotomy, a charade played out well in public but an uninhibited abandon in private. While they were mindful of Frederick's authority, it was sometimes difficult to disassociate him from one of the boys.

The lake was exactly as Stefan had described. In normal times, it would have been packed with campers, fishermen, and sunbathers. Today it stood abandoned, the pristine beach absent of foot prints, void of picnic debris, barking dogs, and smoldering campfires—the ideal setting to get away from the war and forget. And the boys wasted little time shedding their clothes to swim, taking advantage of the abundant solitude. Modesty got cast aside when twenty naked bodies bobbed like penguins in icy water. After a few minutes, Stefan was cornered, stripped, and thrown in the lake, resulting in a boisterous howl from the old one. When the mob finished with Stefan, they charged after Frederick. Their leader attempted to sway them otherwise.

"*Boys*. Boys, you know I am your sergeant. Such folly is not becoming a German leader."

One of the youths yelled out, "Becoming? You will *becoming* wet, Sergeant Freddy."

They seized him against his wishes, laughing all the while, and hoisting him overhead. In a fit of recklessness, they waded into the water and tossed their leader headfirst into the lake. As he hit the water, he dove underneath, swam from behind and began systematically dunking them one at a time.

"The problem with youth," he yelled to Stefan while lashing out in play, "is it is wasted on the young."

Soon Stefan began participating in the lopsided water fight, attempting to rescue his friend. It became all out warfare with those under seventeen versus those over age fifty—two against twenty. Unfortunately for Frederick and Stefan, youth was served.

When the late afternoon sun broke behind trees and Frederick's uniform had dried, he ordered his squad to make preparations to head back to camp. The wind had picked up, switching direction earlier in the day and cooling things off. The change in temperature helped calm the boys' pent-up rambunctiousness. Now, they gathered around a hastily constructed bonfire for warmth and sprawled lazily on the sand, wishing the day could last forever. As they smothered the fire and extinguished its embers, the smoke intensified, rising in long vertical plumes. They watched the wind play with the soot-laden column, swirling it higher and higher until it mixed with the other smoke, the smoke from Stalag 4's secret factory. No one said anything of the surreal sight of the two converging contrails but they all suspected.

(1972)

"Good morning, Zoey."

"You mean, good afternoon."

He pawed a wrist realizing his watch had been left on the nightstand.

"*Afternoon?*"

"Yes, Richard. Afternoon. You slept sixteen hours. I checked you twice to see if you were breathing. You were, so I left you alone. You were exhausted."

He couldn't believe it either. *Sixteen hours*? He suddenly felt an overpowering need to make up for lost time. Stretching his arms above his head, he bent over to touch his toes. His back popped, rattling the saucer and tea cup Zoey was holding. She cringed.

"Yuk."

"Sorry," he apologized. "It's an old injury. I compressed a few vertebrae playing football at the Academy. 'I have to go through this routine every morning or I get spasms."

"I guess I'm not the only one with medical issues," she interjected.

He brushed off her comment, too preoccupied with his stretching. He bent even lower until his hands palmed the floor and the next joint gave way, popping even louder than the first. As he worked on the third vertebra, it occurred to him how he could not remember anything from the night before. He recalled how they managed to find her parent's cottage about the time it got dark. He remembered collapsing on the small twin bed but he could not recall how his shirt and pants vanished, only to become miraculously pressed and starched and folded neatly on the nightstand. He glanced at her again.

"You must have helped me out last night?"

"It was not easy. You were a dead weight. But I did succeed in removing some of your things and cleaning and pressing your uniform." She paused, eyeing his shabby banlon shirt and straight-leg corduroy pant ensemble.

"First time in a while for these old things. A tad dated, aren't they?"

"Not as dated as my father's lederhosen. In case you had no civilian clothes, I was prepared to lend you what was left in his closet," she teased.

"*Lederhosen*?" He cracked a grin.

"I am trying to keep you smiling, Richard. This is my quest. Remember?"

"Won't be easy."

"I can handle it."

He smiled again, this time nervously, not sure if he wanted to be a pet project. "Mind if I have a look around?" He asked, hoping to end their conversation.

"Be my guest but try and be back in ten minutes. I am making us lunch."

This time he feigned a concerted smile, especially as he brushed past her out of the kitchen and into the adjoining den. Once out of sight, his face contorted to the serious business of figuring out why he was there in the first place. Glancing around at his hideaway, he couldn't help but grow curious about his whereabouts.

The cottage, he concluded, appeared more of a getaway—a two bedroom bungalow hidden near the woods; it was ideal for a weekend vacation from the city. It had been built in log cabin style with walls constructed entirely of spruce. There was no ceiling except for the exposed rafters and the inside slope of a shake roof. The layout oozed utilitarian with less than eight hundred square feet of living space. Open and exposed with bedroom and kitchen walls erected after-the-fact, the style troubled him. With all the open space Zoey probably heard him snoring. He walked to the far end of the den, embarrassed by the thought he could have kept her awake. A huge paned window dominated the back wall as did a massive rock chimney in the corner. The window let in enough light that during the day the few electric lights draped overhead need not be turned on. He noticed the den, like his bedroom, had been furnished simply with no bright colors whatsoever, no lavish furnishings, no wall paintings or keepsake mementos, and decorated with Spartan minimalist adornment. He liked it. Even with scant adornments and bland coloring, the place exuded German warmth.

Peering out the window he discovered the cottage sat on the edge of a meadow with the meadow roughly half a kilometer square. Surrounding the meadow lay a vast forest. The cottage reposed like an island surrounded by a sea of grass and spruce. He walked out the back door for a better viewing and drew a breath of fresh air. The sun hit him directly in the face; he guessed his bearing faced south. Strolling down the hill into the meadow, grass and wildflowers brushed past his knees and lured him deeper toward its center. Other than an occasional bird's chirping, the only sounds were the rustlings of his legs through foliage. It was all breathtakingly beautiful and the perfect sanctuary his troubled soul needed.

He bent over and picked a spray of flowers. When he returned, re-climbing the hill, he noticed the exterior of the house had been trimmed in light blue with blue shutters and a neatly arranged set of geranium runners secured under the back picture window. It reminded him of German-styled houses he imagined as a youth in Iowa while listening to his mother read Grimm Brothers fairy tales. He thought his mother would enjoy this house. And he would have stayed outside longer savoring the sights but he guessed his ten minutes had expired, so he stole back inside, carrying the spray as a surprise. "I picked these for you," he said, upon his return. "I thought the old place could use a little color."

"Why, thank you Richard. That is very kind of you," she replied, gathering the flowers and setting them in a vase. "Here. Have a seat. I take it you found the accommodations to your liking?"

"Better than I could have ever imagined. *They're perfect.*"

"Good."

Watching Zoey move throughout the kitchen, he began to notice details about her appearance overlooked earlier and being half-asleep. She looked even more beautiful today than the day before, he concluded. Her blonde hair parted in the middle, braided into two tails looped back on the sides and held in place with light blue ribbons. The ribbons dangled to her shoulders and subtly framed her face. She had selected a white and blue gingham knee-length dress with white apron; a white, short-sleeve blouse puffed at her shoulders making her frail shoulders loom much larger. The blue in the dress matched her eyes and even the trim on the house. Her meticulous attempt at synchronizing colors tickled him. The white knee-high stockings and black patent-leather shoes, the ones with the large brass buckles, completed the old-world wardrobe. She thoroughly captivated him. Such a startling change from the grungy appearance the day before.

"Well, what do you think?" She asked, pointing at the feast on the table.

His eyes remained fixated on her until he realized she had repeated the question a third time, waving her hand in front of his mesmerized face. He attempted to placate his inquisitor by cursorily scanning the table—meats, pancakes, and fruits—before stringing together a few unintelligible consonants. Being verbally flustered in front of a woman had not happened in years, he told himself. "Gee-whiz, this is all nice," he finally eked, "but I feel like I'm about to have lunch with *the St. Pauli girl*."

Zoey laughed at the remark and assured him the St. Pauli girl was mythical, she was not. She encouraged him to sit and eat and remained content to silently watch him consume a stack of pancakes. Likewise, she refrained from asking him questions for fear he might gag while answering. When he finished, she suggested they go for a walk through the meadow and led him out the back door to the secret places she claimed as a little girl.

"So, why the folk dress today? Where are the bell-bottoms, the love beads, the Haight-Ashbury hippie looks?" He asked.

"Gone," she stated straightaway.

"Gone? That's it?"

"Well, Richard, you know the old saying, 'when in Rome, do as the Romans.' This is the Black Forest. I am adapting by wearing my Black Forest dress."

"Do this often?"

"No. I have not worn this old thing in years. It was the only thing left in my closet. I thought it would be fun to wear. That's all. As far as the bell-bottoms and beads, they are like—"

"Ah-h-h, I owe you a new medallion, don't I?" He interrupted.

"Yes, you do. Don't worry. I will let you work it off."

"Chores?"

"Let me finish. My *hippie* wardrobe, as you would call it, is only one side of me. I have many sides." She smiled raising her eyebrows, nodding her head.

"I'm beginning to understand," he replied. "And *Chores*?"

"Yes. If you plan on staying here for any length of time, there is wood needing to be chopped for winter. There are rotted planks needing to be mended. And I know my parents would be greatly obliged to have the trim boards repainted."

"I see. Looks like I have a full agenda."

"It all depends on how long you intend to stay."

A puzzled look came over his face. "Say, I thought you were leaving today?"

"I changed my mind. I decided you were too big of a challenge for me to simply walk away. Besides, who is going to supervise and make sure you are actually doing the chores?"

"Uh-huh. And what do your parents think about all this?"

"They don't know you are here with me. I told them I was bored and decided to spend the night in Freiburg. And that is all they need to know. I'm a big girl."

His mouth puckered, not sure this arrangement was a wise move. He definitely felt uneasy about her not leveling with her parents. And he had hoped to have time to himself. Time with her could prove all-consuming, all-distracting. How was he going to resolve his desertion issue with her hanging around?

"Zoey, I just—"

"I know. I know. You need space."

"Yes, that's part of it."

"And I am in your way. Look, Richard, you never did ask me what I think you should do. Does my opinion not matter?"

"Yes, it matters. So, what do you think I should do?"

"I am glad you *finally* asked." She turned to face him, deliberately capturing his hands and squeezing them until he winced. But what began as a serious moment quickly evaporated, when he noticed the mischievous sparkle in her eyes. "You see," she continued, "I have given your problem serious thought and have come to the conclusion you should stay here the rest of your life, do chores, and be my *slave boy*, in which case you will formally address me as *The Master*. I would much prefer, of course, the equivalent feminine title, *The Mistress*," she proclaimed, lowering her voice to a whisper, "but only in the strictest sense of the words."

He roared in laughter. "You're not helping."

"Sure I am. You just laughed didn't you?"

"Yes, but—"

"No *buts*, Richard. *No regrets*. And, unless I am mistaken, it appears to me my therapy is working." She winked at him.

"Okay, but really, I do need help."

"Well, you have come to the right place. Now, I want you to bow to your mistress and repeat, 'I am your slave boy.' Well, go on. Do it."

"I don't think so. I'm no one's slave. Not yours or the U.S. Army's."

"Hm-m-m-m, well, I guess, in answer to your previous question about what you should do, if I were you I would definitely *not* go back to your base. It seems clear to me that you are not willing to allow someone else to decide your fate. You are your own man, Richard."

"You're right."

She pouted, twisting her face to mimic a little girl. "And I was very much looking forward to having my own little slave boy. Now, whatever shall I do?"

"Pick another game," he retorted.

"Good idea. How does Hansel and Gretel sound?"

"Not that again?"

"Why not?"

"Because—"

"Because you are an old fuddy-duddy?"

"Hey, I can't be more than six or seven years older than you. I'm no fuddy-duddy. I have a lot on my mind, that's all."

"Hansel, look around you. Have you no idea where you are? You are in the Black Forest. You are in the *enchanted forest* where anything is possible and where dreams come true. If you cannot forget your problems here, where can you forget them?"

"I know, but—"

She pushed him on the ground.

"Remember what I said. *No buts—no regrets.* Tag. You are it, Hansel."

She ran away, laughing. He jumped up, brushed himself

off, and tore after her.

"Now you're really in trouble *Gretel*."

(2000)

When the doorbell rang for the tenth time he tried to ignore the clatter but it would not let up. Mitchell Jameson cursed, having to stop mid-sentence in his typing.

"Stop ringing the doorbell. I'm coming."

He limped to the door with a desk chair imprinted on his backside, almost forgetting he had spent the entire day pecking away on the laptop. He forgot he was wearing nothing but two-day old boxer shorts and a smelly T-shirt. Why bother dressing? He didn't have to go out again for three days, to his next counseling session. He had plenty of food stashed in the freezer. But somewhere enroute to the door, he forgot his manners, being preoccupied by an excellent day of writing and, now, stood unshaven and exposed half-naked in the doorway—*to his wife*.

"Susan. What are you doing here?"

"I came to see you. I was worried. I called but no one answered. I had all these crazy thoughts racing through my head. Did he shoot himself? Is he dead? Is he hurt?"

"No, no, I'm alright."

They stared at each other, both uncomfortable with the situation.

"You don't look good, Mitchell."

"I've been writing. You know how I get when I'm in a groove."

"It's been a while since that happened, hasn't it?"

"Yes."

"Harvey told me you were writing again. It's a good sign. Right?"

"Yes. I think it is." He paused to study her face. She looked tired. Her eyes were bloodshot and she appeared gaunter than a week earlier. Her dress, which undoubtedly fit her at one time, draped loosely on her shoulders. And her hands trembled out of control. Suddenly, he felt guilty, again. After all, he caused her torment and this unannounced visit to Colorado. "Come in, Susan. Don't stand out there. Come," he pleaded, waving her inside.

Even before she stepped in, tears welled in her eyes. Standing on the threshold, she was tempted to turn around and run. The center of her life, the man she worshiped, had abandoned her for another woman and the pain had grown unbearable. Looking at him looking at her, she sensed failure as a human being. Doubts and self-blame tormented her thoughts to the brink of madness: Why didn't he love her enough to stay in Austin? What pushed him away in their relationship? How did she manage to lose him? Yet, for all the questions, there were no answers. All she wanted was the old Mitchell back, the one she had fallen in love with—not this man. This man she did not know. This man was a stranger. And it would have been far easier to deal with his death than all of this. Death at least has closure but not infidelity. Infidelity has a memory with no ending and its aftermath is far worse—separation, divorce, and a broken heart which never mends. Her heart needed to be told it was loved and how the whole ghastly affair had been a mistake. If he had just talked to her, everything would have been better. But that's not the course he chose. He chose to implode and bury the world inside his head and wallow in self-pity, solving his own problems because *he was a man*. It's what men do, she thought. It's what they learn from their fathers and their father's father: Don't show emotion. Don't show pain. Don't show weakness. And, above all else, keep it bottled tightly inside. She thought her job was to be the sounding board for his self-doubts, the sponge for his worries, the steadfast love for his soul until death do us part. But Mitchell wouldn't allow her the consolation. He had to do it his way, by himself, and she didn't understand any of what was going on. Now, in spite of the mess he created, she swallowed her pride and stepped over the threshold.

"I'm sorry, Susan. I unplugged the phone. I guess that was a pretty selfish thing to do, huh?"

"Yes. It was."

He felt like an idiot with no idea how to respond. Feelings of shame resurfaced. These were the same feelings that drove him to flee to Colorado in the first place. They were the same feelings he had been unable to shake—far easier to concentrate on small talk, he reasoned. Far easier to avoid the reason why he left home and had an affair and jettisoned his family. He paused to search for anything to avoid the awkward silence. "Did you drive here or fly?" He finally uttered.

"I flew to Denver. I rented a car at the airport."

He pointed to the couch. "Have a seat. Would you like something to drink? Eat?"

"I can't eat. The past few days I've been vomiting every time I try. I went to the doctor. He gave me pills." She buried her face in her hands and began to sob. "I'm going crazy,

Mitchell. My world, *our world*, is falling apart."

He sat next to her. "Please don't cry, Susan. It's not your fault. I did this to you. I'm the one who cheated. I'm the one who ran out. I'm the one who has problems. That's why I'm here. I'm getting counseling twice a week. I think my counselor is going to be able to help me. To help *us* through this."

"Then, answer me honestly, Mitchell. Will we ever be a family again? The girls constantly ask about you. Your father keeps calling. I can't count the times. He's very worried. He said this all started after your mother's death and you rummaged through a trunk in their attic. Have you thought about that—how maybe you snapped or something?"

"I've thought about a lot of things but the bottom line is I have no one to blame but myself. I made bad choices. I handled things poorly."

"Have you talked to *her* since you've been here?"

"No."

"Honestly?"

He put his hand over his heart. "Honest. The doctor told me never to think or mention the *bitch's* name again."

"She called her a bitch?"

"Yup."

"I like your doctor already," she said, attempting to wipe away tears.

"Me, too."

He put his arm around her. She laid her head on his shoulder.

"Susan, I love you. I don't want us to ever go through this again. I know there are things we need to work on. And I know I need to do a better job sharing feelings with you but I don't want to blow it again. I don't want to make another mistake. I want to get at the root of the problem. Until that's done, I can't come home."

"I understand. I don't like it Mitchell but I understand."

They said nothing for minutes but held each other. Finally, she broke the silence." Do you ever think of me Mitchell, while you're here? While you're writing?"

"All the time," he stated, turning to look at her. "Remember when we went skinny-dipping in the lake outside Grapevine? When we got drunk on peach schnapps and built the bonfire to stay warm? Remember you said I looked like a penguin bobbing in water?"

"Yes, I remember."

"Well," he said, shrugging his shoulders, "bits and pieces of our history are in this story. *Bits and pieces of us*."

"You didn't?"

"Hey, it would be hard not to write about our lives, Susan. How can I leave out the most important parts of us in any of my writing? Like the weekend we stayed at your parent's cabin in the Hill Country? Remember *the game*?" He grinned.

"When we played *Hansel and Gretel*?" She gasped.

"Yup."

"You didn't?" She hit his chest with the flat of her hand.

"Uh-huh."

She looked at him and instinctively brushed back matted hair on his forehead. "I like it when you smile, Mitchell. I'm going to make it one of my projects from now on—to see more smiles from you."

He could live with her love, he told himself. He could even write about it.

FOUR
(1945)

The air raid sirens wailed for a second time. For over a week, bombs dropped closer to the post. One had scored a misguided hit on the factory a few nights earlier, shutting down production and vanquishing the smokestacks. Frederick couldn't understand why Allied bombers struck so close to a POW camp, especially with red crosses painted clearly on the tops of the chimneys.

Concerned more than ever about the approaching Allied armies, Frederick and Stefan bought a radio from fleeing Panzer troops to uncover the truth about the war. That night they were eager to tune in the broadcast out of Berlin, the first time the small wireless had been tested. Huddled around the device, they hoped to learn about the worsening situation but Allied jamming made listening impossible.

"Frederick, shall I tune in the BBC? I know we can pick it up. You speak English. Yeah?"

Frederick had always been loath to listen to the enemy, let alone the enemy's propaganda on Germany's current state. He had heard from troops headed to the front how American First and Third armored units had struck to the south and were moving into the Rhone valley. How the fight had turned into an all-out effort to defend the Fatherland. Freiburg had been taken without a shot fired as retreating divisions fell back to regroup—always regrouping but never fighting. The Russians were knocking on Berlin's door. Now the British and Canadians were slicing through the Netherlands and threatening Germany's northwest border. He wasn't sure if he wanted to listen to disinformation from the enemy to confirm his worst fears. But the radio reports out of Berlin were, indeed, being jammed and he decided any news was better than no news. Besides, the plight of Lili and his son consumed his thoughts. Maybe they had been spared the worst, he hoped.

"Go ahead," he agreed.

"Good. They play Benny Goodman. You like him. Yeah?

"No," he replied, "but Lili does."

Stefan found the frequency and the two listened to lively music. It wasn't long before the boys in the adjoining room also heard the tunes and left their bunks, gathering around the radio one-by-one, sitting cross-legged in a circle campfire-style on the barrack's dank wooden floor. For a solid hour they were able to take advantage of the lull in the aerial bombardment and enjoy the rare solitude of the evening by getting lost in the music and thinking about loved ones. Frederick lit his pipe, the first time in weeks. He sensed this particular evening with his new family was as close as he would ever get to the real thing.

When the news bulletin broke, the group asked their leader if he could translate the broadcast. Like most things his boys wanted, it was hard for him to say 'No.' How could he deny his *children*? He listened closely to the words and paraphrased in German as best he could:

. . .*NEWS FLASH—Montgomery's heroic forces have crossed the Ems River and are less than twenty miles from Bremen. Our brave lads have met little resistance as the Nazi war machine retreats for one last stand to save Germany's northwest border . . . .*

"They say the British army has crossed the Ems River.

They're closing in on us, dear lads. It does not sound good." He puffed nervously as pipe smoke swirled above his head and out the window.

. . .German forces are taking a pounding and falling back. Over one-hundred thousand soldiers of the once elite Panzer Second Division have been taken prisoner in the south by the U.S. Army's Third . . . .

"They claim many of our soldiers have surrendered. You cannot believe everything they say. They want us to give up. They want to hurt our morale."

"They lie. Yeah?" Stefan asked.

"Most likely."

. . .Reports of war atrocities continue to filter in as early expeditionary forces uncover more detention factories in guise as POW camps. From Auschwitz, eyewitnesses describe mass graves where as many as eight hundred thousand Jews have been systematically tortured to death by the ruthless Nazi Gestapo . . . .

One of the boys spoke up.

"I recognized the name Auschwitz. I live not too far from there. What did they say, Sergeant Freddy?"

"Sh-h-h-h. Quiet." He insisted.

. . .while tens of thousands more were deliberately starved in concentration camps, carnage the likes of which humanity has never seen. It is reported that many survivors were shipped north to other camps before Allied forces could liberate them . . . .

Frederick got a sickened look on his face. He reached over and turned off the radio.

"Well, what did they say?" the same boy persisted, his face

seized with worry.

"Nothing of importance," Frederick shrugged. "They say the area has been captured by the Americans. That is all. Nothing of casualties. I'm sure everything is fine. The Americans will treat your people with respect. Now it is time to sleep. Everyone go to bed. That's an order."

He stood to excuse himself, stumbling out the back door before anyone could read his face and interpret his anguish. The door's screened frame slammed behind him; twenty pairs of eyes watched him run to the fence and peer toward Section A.

His children would never understand, he thought. And he didn't want them to. What sane world sends children to war to execute other children? He wondered. Of course, there was no answer. He desperately wanted one; he wanted to trust Germany, his honorable Germany, the old Germany of the Kaiser. What will be left for us to believe in if my suspicions are right? He fretted. If he could run away from it all, he surely would. And if he could sneak the boys out and never look back, he would surely do that, too. He turned around and stared at the barrack lights. They had begun singing, rallying for the moment with their voices heard by the same people who caused human ashes to litter Germany's skies. They were singing his and Lili's song:

> *Underneath the lantern by the barrack gate,*
> *Darling I remember the way you used to wait;*
> *'Twas there that you whispered tenderly,*
> *That you loved me,*
> *You'd always be,*
> *My Lili of the lamplight,*
> *My own Lili Marlene . . . .*

Frederick never slept that night. Stefan found him standing by the same stockade fence, still looking in toward Section A.

"Freddy, I keep hearing terrible rumors about what is going on inside there," Stefan said, pointing toward the factory.

"These times thrive on rumors, Stefan," Frederick replied. "Ignore them. The enemy will say anything to discredit Germany and make us quit believing in ourselves and our virtues."

"I agree but I cannot ignore this. Here. See for yourself," he replied, holding out a bag of poison—*rat poison.* "I was told to add this to the borscht today, by order of our illustrious commandant. Why would the commandant want me to poison the inmates' food? Is it a joke? A mistake?"

In disbelief, Frederick tore open the bag. He smelled the pellets.

"*Brodifacoum.* How many of these were you given to put in the food?"

"There are nine more bags. They are stacked in the kitchen awaiting your orders."

"Nine?"

"Yeah."

"Nine bags? That does not make sense. There is not enough to . . . unless—"

"Unless?"

"Unless it is not meant to—" He eyed Stefan without finishing.

"*What?*"

"Meant to kill. Brodifacoum shuts down the central nervous system. It can stop the heart. In something as small as a rat or animal with a high metabolism it kills. But in lower dosages, in humans, it calms and soothes, especially if the metabolism has already been slowed."

"Slowed by starvation?" Stefan pressed.

"Yes, if that was the case. As far as we officially know, no one has starved here."

"But it could work like a sedative?"

"Yes, sort of."

"Hm-m-m-m. Why would he want the workers calmed?"

"Stefan, don't ask me anymore questions and do not tell anyone about this. Do as you are told. Add the poison. *It won't kill anyone*." Frederick sighed. "Tell the boys we are having a secret meeting at midnight in my quarters. Everyone is required to be there. Understood?"

"Yes, but I don't think—"

"*Just do it*. Follow orders for once, Stefan. <u>Don't think</u>."

(1972)

When he caught up with her, Zoey had collapsed on the ground in the middle of the meadow. He was panting heavily and not quite sure how such a petite creature could have outpaced him for five straight minutes. He always thought himself a good sprinter and in decent condition but every time he got close enough to tag her, *Gretel* managed to duck underneath his reach. He finally pleaded with her to slow down. Perspiration now dripped from his face and onto his shirt, drenching it. He collapsed on a thick mat of grass and wildflowers, and remained content to simply capture his breath.

"You don't follow orders, do you, Zoey?" He panted.

"That is not my nature nor yours, *Hansel*," she winked. "Besides, I am not the one in the military."

Richard didn't respond. He was too exhausted. Instead, he took advantage of the lull by checking out the lush surroundings and permitting his senses to relish the afternoon. It was heavenly there, isolated from the rest of the world and its problems. It reminded him of a field in Iowa where he played hooky and drank beer with his buddies on Friday afternoons—peaceful, sheltering, secretive. Zoey protected him far more than his pals back in Iowa, he told himself. They always got him into trouble—the nature of the teenage male. Not Zoey. She was more like a guardian angel sent to protect and rescue him from this latest turmoil.

That spectacular August day paradise belonged solely to them—but even heaven had limitations. Heaven would never reek of body odor. And he couldn't stand the smell on his banlon shirt, so he removed it and used the cloth to wipe off his face and chest.

"I hope this doesn't offend you?" He asked, throwing the shirt over a shoulder. *"I'm hotter than Hades."*

"No, not at all," she replied, studying his physique and eyeing the series of scars strung across his chest. "What are those?" She asked, eyeing the injuries.

"Old wounds. Caused by bone fragments. A land mine exploded, blowing my lieutenant's legs off. His calf shredded to pieces. The bones tore me up."

She grimaced. "That had to be horrible."

"Yes, it was. But fortunately, we got him medevacked right away. He beat the odds—made it. Now practices law in

Chicago. We write to each other all the time. He's a big peace advocate. Works with Abby Hoffman and a bunch of other activists. He's been encouraging me to go to Switzerland."

"Do you think you will go? Go to Switzerland?"

"Probably. Maybe. Ask me in another week."

"*Another week?*"

"Yeah. I like it here. What's the rush? Right?"

She hesitated before saying anything, wanting him to make a stand and not capitulate to his orders. She wanted him to question the moral soundness of the war his superiors wanted him to fight, a war she abhorred.

"Look, Richard, what I said earlier about you staying here. I meant every word of it. You can stay as long as you want. You don't have to go to Switzerland."

"I appreciate your hospitality, Zoey, but I'm not sure if I want to be this far from my son. If I decide to seek amnesty there's always Canada, or, or. . ." he stammered.

"Or?"

"Or that other option."

"I hope you do not mean Vietnam. That is no option."

He wrinkled his nose. "Even if I do, there are ways of keeping your head down, laying low out of harm's way if you want to badly enough. Don't forget, this is the profession I chose. Nobody said being a peacekeeper would be easy."

"Your Vietnam is not an honorable war."

"Are there any?"

"Probably not," she replied, realizing she had little sway over his final decision. Ultimately, she decided whatever the outcome, the decision had to be one he could live with and abruptly changed the subject. "Richard, you mentioned yesterday you thought the man buried at the cemetery might be your father. What made you say that? Why all the mystery?"

"It's not a matter of what I *say*, Zoey. It's a matter of what I *know*." He paused leaning forward to gather a handful of grass and began sorting through the stems. He selected one, placing a tasseled reed in his mouth, chomping until it crunched between his teeth. He leaned back to rest on his elbows without looking at her. "You see, I'm adopted. Who my real parents are is the mystery. It's why I'm here."

"There has got to be more to the story, Richard. Don't you want to talk to me about it? I am a good listener."

"I know you are. And you've been good, helping me so far. I suppose the least I can do is share what drew me to Freiburg."

He sat straight and swiveled to face her, tucking his legs underneath cross-legged. She knew she was in for a story and mimicked his gesture. Their knees touched.

"My parents, the parents who adopted me, that is, rescued me from a refugee camp run by the American Red Cross in January, 1946, after the war. I'm told the camp wasn't too far from Freiburg. I was only two or three at the time, but nobody knew exactly how old I was. Apparently, nothing was known of my biological parents or my real identity. The story goes, I was found abandoned and wandering through the camp crying. It was one of the coldest winters in Europe. No one had any food. The nurses felt sorry for me and took me in. My only possession—a butterfly shadow box, a collector's box, had been slung around my neck. It was as though somebody wanted me to always have it as a keepsake of who I was, of my past. The man we looked up, the one at the cemetery, Frederick VonObst, his name was written in the corner of the box's mounting board. I've always assumed my past is linked to his. He may or may not be my father. It was all I had to go on, Zoey."

"How did your parents find you?"

"The newspapers in Iowa carried the story. They called me 'The Butterfly Boy.' My parents saw my picture. They said it was 'love at first sight.' They always wanted a son, so they pursued adoption, and, well, the rest, as they say, is history. Being a toddler at the time, I don't remember any of it. I just know I was lucky to have been taken in by such generous loving people. And I really appreciate my parents and what they did. I can't imagine growing up anywhere but Iowa or in the United States, for that matter. Maybe it's why I always wanted to join the military—because I've always felt like I owed America something. And, now, I want to find out if my biological parents are still alive. Is discovering the truth a bad thing?"

"No, not at all." She held his hand again. "And you don't remember anything, Richard?"

"No. Every now and then I have these flashbacks. I picture a woman. She's beautiful and she sings to me and runs her fingers through my hair. I think she is my mother but it's more dreamlike than anything else. No, I don't remember much. I thought coming here would help. Seems pointless, now, doesn't it?"

"You never know?" She grinned.

"Know what?"

"You are German. I am German. We could be related."

"Oh, brother. That's a scary thought."

She placed her second hand over his. "I don't think so. I don't think so at all."

By the end of the week they were running out of supplies. Zoey said she would *drive* into town to buy groceries. Her wardrobe of bell-bottom jeans and traditional folk dresses had been exhausted; she wanted to go shopping for new clothes and, more importantly, had her parent's credit card. He said he would accompany her, that he was experiencing cabin fever and wanted to sightsee. Suddenly, he did a double-take recalling her exact words. "*Drive?* Drive what?" He asked. She motioned for him to follow her and led him to a dilapidated barn he had yet to explore. Her parents kept a car stashed inside, she said, a "little runabout." It's an old relic, she insisted. Besides, there were far too many cars at the estate in Frankfurt. This one, she quipped, was nothing more than a spare kept in storage for emergencies. It had been hidden away in the musty barn under a tarp.

She unloosened the draw strings and pulled back the cover. The *old relic* happened to be a classic '60 Porsche Targa convertible, a Bavarian cream color with scooped rear engine spoiler and signature rounded profile. For a second or two his heart leaped from his chest. It was the exact car he dreamt about as a youth and always got him in trouble with the local import dealer when he sat in the driver's seat of the showroom model and pretended to be racing at Lemans, (unsuspectingly stripping the gears). He salivated. His dream machine sat in front of him in all its resplendent glory. He stared at it, mouth agape. After a few minutes of gawking, he helped Zoey fold the ragtop, the only visible sign of the Porsche's age, never once taking his eyes off the car. He ran his hands over its body, feeling every crevice, touching the well-engineered moldings, taking more time to fondle it than Margaret McElvenny his high school heartthrob.

Zoey glared at Richard.

"What's wrong?" He asked.

"I feel like a voyeur. Are you finished making love?"

He grinned sheepishly. "Only if I can drive it."

She tossed him the keys. He immediately jumped over the door and slid into the driver's seat. He hadn't done that move in over twelve years. He felt the leather appointments and touched the knobs and gauges. Nothing had changed. He reached over and unlatched her door, almost forgetting she stood there impatiently tapping her foot.

"Hot damn. Just the way I remember, Zoey." He giggled.

"I take it you have done this before, Richard."

"*Oh. Yeah.*"

He cranked the engine. It took three tries before it fired. He patiently fed its thirsty injectors gas. Within a minute it purred to his liking. He revved the engine to 5000 RPM, cleaning out its carburetor and, without advance warning, popped the clutch unleashing its 180 horsepower. The car leaped out of the barn fishtailing wildly, spraying dirt, straw, and bits of gravel everywhere. When they reached the end of the driveway, he slammed on the brakes, skidding to a halt inches short of the highway.

Zoey gave him a dirty look, moving her head back and forth, checking for signs of whiplash. He ignored her and began fumbling, instead, with the radio until he found a Jan and Dean tune—*Dead Man's Curve*. He turned up the volume. She groaned.

"Which way to Freiburg?" He asked, laughing out loud like a giddy schoolboy.

The laughter pleased Zoey. He, at least, was having a good time. She pointed to the right. He turned left. Ten seconds later they were flying down the narrow back roads of the Black Forest at one hundred twenty kilometers an hour.

(2000)

"What are you thinking about, Mitchell?"

"An old song." He began humming the melody out loud.

"Ah-huh. I don't recognize it. What is it?"

"An old tune by Jan and Dean. Remember *Dead Man's Curve?*"

"I thought you said you liked the old ballad stuff. What was the one last week?"

"*Lili Marlene* by Marlene Dietrich."

"That's right. I couldn't remember the title. Why that one?" She asked, her voice muffled by curtains.

The change in her voice aroused his curiosity. He turned sideways on the couch to see what was going on. Even after a full minute's gaze, she didn't realize he was staring at her, being preoccupied peering through the window and more interested in parking lot commotion than what he had to say. He shook his head in disgust deciding to sit up.

"It seems to calm me right before I take a poop."

"Nice," she replied, still looking out the window.

"Laura, did you hear what I said?"

"Uh-huh. You like to poop to Marlene Dietrich songs."

"Laura. *Laura, look at me.*"

She turned around, embarrassed he caught her not concentrating on his every word.

"I'm sorry, Mitchell, I heard a car alarm or something. It distracted me."

He held up the flat of both palms, looking at the floor. "It's okay. You don't need to apologize. I'm bored, too."

"You are?"

"Yes."

She grabbed her tablet and began to scrawl, talking out loud in monotone. "Session five and patient is already bored."

He laughed, shaking his head, offended by her style. "Listen to yourself. You're worse than me."

"And how do you figure?"

"For starters, you're just going through the motions here, collecting a check to pay for your new Porsche. Listen, I don't feel any better about my situation than I did when we began."

"Actually, you're the one going through the motions—not me."

"Oh? You think?"

"Look. These are *your* sessions, not mine. If you were completely wacko or nutty as a fruitcake, it'd all be different—the way these little get get-togethers of ours would be conducted. But you're not crazy or unbalanced. You're just a little nuts like the rest of us. So, my job is to facilitate *your feelings*. To keep *you* focused on target for the objective. After all, you're the one who has to solve the problem."

"Are we on target?"

"Hm-m-m-m, let's see . . . on target? Hm-m-m-m, we've

talked about such a variety of different topics, I've lost track," she stated sarcastically, tapping her pen. "First, there was the long-winded discussion about your parents and your siblings. We concluded they're all screwed up. What else is new? Welcome to the post- *Father Knows Best* generation. After that, we talked about your fascination for female breasts and how your uncle started you on a downward spiral when he exposed you to Playboy magazines at the impressionable age of nine. Then, we ventured into your Irritable Bowel Syndrome and traced it to your mother's potty training efforts and the jelly beans she rewarded you for firm 'doogies.' You mentioned you still have the Bavarian cream-colored childhood toilet seat in your closet, the one with the cute rubber duck head that squeaks irresistibly when squeezed. Apparently as a child you squeaked it a great deal earning you the adorable reputation as 'the jelly bean baby.' I do find most of that relatively distasteful." She paused to take a swallow of Perrier, swishing it in her mouth and obnoxiously wiping her lips with a shirt sleeve. "Let's see, where was I? Oh, yes, the *doogy years*. Next we jumped forward to your high school testosterone interest, a Miss Margaret McIvy or McElvenny or some other forgettable name. You said she loved the way you fondled her in the back seat of her father's European sports car. I believe we spent the entire fourth session on that topic. You went into great detail describing your sexual prowess and how you were God's gift to female delayed orgasm. Yes, those were the exact words. I remember our session very clearly because it was the same day I threw up as soon as you left my office."

He became visibly irritated. "Look, you don't need to insult me. I get the message."

"Do you? Don't I? Well, here's a news flash for you—*we're not getting anywhere*. I still haven't a clue why you left Susan or what motivated you to have an affair in the first place. Frankly, I'm getting tired of all this. Aren't you?"

"Yes, but—"

"No buts here, Mitchell, or regrets. Only the truth counts here. Only what's relevant is important. So, when do we get there? I'm holding my breath until something of value exhumes from that semi-intelligent but highly-suppressed mouth of yours." She puffed her cheeks and crossed her eyes. He said nothing. After a few seconds passed, she frantically pointed to her bulging cheeks while pretending to pass out.

"Alright. Alright. Jesus, you're weird. You win."

She exhaled. "Thank God."

He made a sour face and, without forethought, capitulated to her original question. "I got involved with the other woman because I was looking for an escape."

"From what?"

"From everything. From my past. From my problems with Susan. From the lies. From everything reminding me of who I wasn't. The other woman became an easy target." He paused to collect his thoughts. "Oh, brother was she ever easy. *Easy* in every sense of the word. She was looking for someone to latch onto. Anyone, including the successful literary writer, Mitchell Jameson, the married man with two little girls. She didn't care if I was married. She wanted a man. A man preferably loaded with cash. And, for your information, she didn't manipulate me. *We* manipulated each other to our own ends. She became my escape. My way of not dealing with problems."

"I take it you're not blaming her entirely for the

infidelity?"

"No. A little, perhaps. I mean, it's not as if she wasn't aware of what she was doing. She played me. Truth is, I allowed myself to get manipulated. Heck, if it wasn't her, it would have been someone else. It was just a matter of time. I was an accident waiting to happen."

"*So. . . .*"

"So?"

"So, what are you saying, *Grasshopper?*"

As she asked the question, her eyes squinted, her head cocked to the side. He looked at her, a little confused.

"I guess what I'm saying, or actually doing is taking responsibility for my own actions. I can't blame anyone or anything but myself—not Susan. Not my mother and the doogy syndrome. Not my uncle and the booby magazines. Only myself for not confronting my problems head-on."

"It's about time."

"Think so?"

"Yes. And it's a good start," she stated, pausing to jot more notes. "But, you keep mentioning *your problems*. I think you used the words, 'the lies.' What's that mean?"

"The standard marriage problem stuff. Lies you tell each other."

"I don't think so. You're bullshitting me, again. Knock it off."

"Okay, try this lie on for size: My wife openly admits I'm not the most important person in her life, that the girls are her first priority. I'm relegated to good old number two but only *if* there's any time left over, *if* she doesn't have a headache and isn't too tired and *if* her mind isn't too cluttered with ballet, piano, PTO, and soccer."

"Blah, blah, blah . . . grow up."

"Huh?"

"That's not a lie. That's reality. What do you expect? She's a mother, for Pete's sake. She's taking her responsibility seriously. Isn't it one of the ten reasons why you married Susan in the first place—because you knew she'd be a great mother for your children? I mean, what's the alternative? Be a bad lazy mother who doesn't give a damn? Put all the responsibility on you? Look, she's willing to put her career on hold to provide your children the nurturing you got as a child in Texas. Isn't that what you wanted?"

"Yes, but—"

"No buts here."

"Okay. Right."

"Good. I'm still curious. *When* did she first make this shocking testament, this telltale confession you were merely number two in her life?"

"You mean the very first time?"

"Yes, the very first time."

"A couple of years ago."

"A *couple* of years ago?"

"Yes."

"Hm-m-m. Really? It took you a couple of years to let this anger fester before you actually exploded one day, completely out of the blue, completely in violation of Mitchell Jameson's moral righteous character? All of a sudden your little head went fully erect and pointed south?"

"That's right."

"Uh-huh."

"Scouts honor"

"I don't think so. The revelation you were number two may have been a factor, maybe even a major factor, but I think we still have something else out there we haven't hit upon. Something else that reared four or five months ago—maybe the proverbial straw breaking the camel's back. Care to venture there?"

"No. I mean, there is nothing else. Nowhere else to venture," he replied, trying to change the subject. "And you can't imagine how her words tore me up. How it angered me when she told me straight to my face. I mean, it was already pretty self-evident. All you had to do was look at how she prioritized her life. She didn't need to actually tell me to my face. It was wrong. It hurt."

"Of course it hurt. Life hurts. Big deal. Hey, as the girls grow older, you'll regain the throne again, King Mitchell. Don't get so crazed. It's not forever, you know."

"I know."

"Then, deal with it. *Talk* to Susan. Tell her your feelings. Any woman who is willing to take you back after you've broken your marriage vows, who's willing to tolerate you not living at home while you search for truth, justice, and the American way for months on end, any woman who's willing to do all that, loves you very much. And let me tell you something else," she lowered her voice to a whisper, "with all your doogy-booby fixations, you're not such a great catch, money or not."

"Gee, thanks a bunch, Laura."

"How 'bout we call it a session. Next time I want us to focus on what was going on in your life a few months ago, even though I know you don't want to. I want to find the proverbial straw. Is it a deal?"

"Deal."

"Good. I just think that we—" She stopped midsentence and noticed for the first time how pale he looked. "Mitchell, are you getting out at all these days?"

"Out? A little, I guess. To the store on errands. Gotta drive the car every now and then. But," he sighed, "mostly, I've been holed up writing."

"Hm-m-m-m."

"No, no I'm fine. Honest. I'm cool with it. The writing keeps my mind busy. It's what I do."

"Uh-huh. You need to get out more."

"No, I frigging don't."

"Yes, you *frigging* do. Look, I'm heading over to the club at 6:00 to meet friends. Why don't you join me? You can have a few drinks, unwind, meet some people and actually carry on a conversation. It'll do you good."

"If I go, you won't introduce me as your patient, will you?"

"No. Actually, everyone in the old club has seen me at one time or another. I'm sure they'll put one and one together. It's not a big deal. So what do you say?"

"Well, I can tell you won't take 'No' for an answer."

"You got that right."

"Sure. What the heck. What's the name of the place?"

"O'Keefe's."

"Sounds like an artist pub or something. I could use a drink. It's a date. See you at 6:00."

FIVE
(1945)

"Is it midnight?" One of the boys asked.

"Yes," another replied.

"Good. I have not been able to sleep. Let's go."

They slithered from their bunks, stumbling over unseen objects in the pitch black barrack and tiptoed into the adjoining sleeping quarter of their leader, Sergeant Frederick VonObst. Feeling the floor for a vacant place to sit, they were the last to assemble in the crowded unlit room. Stefan and eighteen others were already huddled together listening to the scratchy sound from the wireless, the music soothing troubled thoughts and assuaging anxieties in these waning days of the war.

"Now everyone is here," Stefan whispered. "What is all the mystery, Freddy?"

Frederick hadn't slept in over thirty-six hours and it showed. Even the moon casting a glow through the window and illuminating his silhouette couldn't hide the fact he was a wreck. His hands trembled.

"Thank you all for coming," he softly spoke. "I know many of you have questions. I may not be able to provide all the answers. Nevertheless, there are things I feel we must discuss. Things considered too secret to discuss openly. I am sure you have all heard rumors about the true nature of this place. We have all tried to ignore such notions, believing in our hearts the unthinkable could not be taking place right here under our noses. It is now time to discuss these things and decide what needs to be done."

One of the boys raised his hand. "Sergeant Freddy, most of us have heard the workers here are Jews and there may be five times the number we thought were living in Section A. Is it true?"

"I cannot confirm it. I have not been permitted beyond the commandant's house. I have only seen a few inmates from a distance. What I have seen, however, is disturbing. I have seen mothers with their small children by their sides. They appeared to be either undernourished or sick."

Another spoke up.

"Everyone here knows the food we have been preparing all these months is only enough for ten thousand prisoners. If there actually are fifty thousand, it would seem we have been slowly starving them to death."

A third spoke out before Freddy could respond. "I have even heard they take the dead ones and burn their bodies in the furnaces. All the smoke from the chimneys is human soot."

The others began to stir, their tongues wagging non-stop. Soon the whispers became heated as the voices raised in horror.

"Quiet everyone. Quiet." Stefan blurted, attempting to silence their outrage.

"I know nothing of this," Frederick pleaded, motioning them to be still for fear of being overheard by passing sentries. "Unfortunately, there have been reports on the radio of other camps like this one that the Americans have uncovered. There are many gruesome stories being told. Things that if true could bring dishonor to Germany. I hope it is simply propaganda to demoralize us and make us want to surrender. It could be, for example, the majority of the workers just happen to be Jews because their lot is typically comprised of anarchists and communists. Everyone knows Jews undermine Germany. They are the ones who would attempt to overthrow our government and poison our Arian culture. It only makes sense they would comprise most of our inmate population. But—"

"*But?*" One of the youths pursued. "Please, no 'buts' here, tonight, Sergeant Freddy. We only want the truth."

"Very well." He sighed. "Rounding up anarchists and communists who would attempt to destabilize Germany's war efforts is one thing, *but* deliberately starving them to death, starving women and small children, is another. *And* I have no reason to suspect the Americans of lying. Lying is not their nature. Therefore, I have concluded this place is unholy—a disgrace to Germany."

Stefan buried his head. A few of the boys began to sob. Others were stunned into silence. They had been taught the virtues of German decency years earlier as children in the Hitler Youth camps and programmed to believe in their country's honor. Certainly their kind was not capable of such atrocities. But tonight they could no longer look the other way and pretend the truth was a lie—*the lie was the truth*. The paradox of this war would become a nightmare from which they would never escape nor their children, nor their children's children.

"What do we do now?" Another boy asked.

"Leave," Frederick replied. "*We get the hell out of here.*"

"But how, Freddy?" Stefan interjected. "We are prisoners as much as those in Section A. We cannot simply march out. How shall we get past the guards? We need paperwork. We need orders. They still shoot deserters. Yeah?"

"I am aware of that, Stefan. But they also shoot *murderers*. The fact is we need to leave as quickly as possible. My best guess is Stalag 4 will fall to the enemy in a matter of days. Do you want to be left to the mercy of the enemy? Do you want to be captured here? Do you want these children to be blamed for what has gone on? This insanity must end, my friend. It is time to go home and to ask God for forgiveness."

Stefan stood and walked to the window. He looked at the moon. The noise from the artillery barrage off in the distance couldn't distract the beauty of the clear night sky. He sensed the camaraderie discovered at the post the past months would all too soon crash to a bitter ending. He moaned out loud, resigned to the idea they were no longer going to be a team. He would miss being part of something and being useful. It saddened him. If they could somehow manage to escape and get out undetected, it meant tonight would be their last evening together. Perhaps, there was one last thing he could do. "I will pack us all bratwurst sandwiches. Yeah?"

"Yes, Stefan. Sandwiches would be good. We have a long difficult journey in front of us." Frederick stated.

"What do you propose, Sergeant Freddy?" One of the youth asked. "I mean, how will we get out?"

"Tomorrow morning a Red Cross truck is bringing supplies for the inmates. It will probably be the last time it comes to this post. We will take advantage of the delivery. When no one is looking, we will stow away in the back of its bed. Once we get far enough away from this place, we will jump out and hide in the woods until the British have captured the valley. Once they control the area, it will be safe for us to move around in the open. I understand there are now so many of us, the British are no longer taking prisoners. You need only wear a white armband to signify you have surrendered. Then, it will be time to return to your loved ones. It may be a long walk home but homesick legs have a way of shortening the journey. Yes?"

The boy smiled. "Yeah. My mother makes the best strudel in the world. I can taste it now." He licked his lips savoring the memory

"Ah-h-h, but is it as good as my bratwurst sandwich?" Stefan egged.

"No, Stefan," they replied in unison. *"Nothing is better than your bratwurst."*

(1972)

The only reason they pulled an about-face and drove to Freiburg was to fill up with petrol. The Porsche's gauge already read empty when they pulled out on the highway but Richard disregarded the warning indicator. Zoey finally talked him into returning to town. She told him there was a hairline crack in the gas line near the fuel injector. The "old thing", as she erroneously referred to the Porsche, always had trouble keeping a full tank. He ignored her badgering at first but, later, agreed, especially when the car began to sputter on curves. Now they were coasting to the pump and he felt a tad guilty.

"Why is it you men always try to squeeze the last drop out of a car's tank?"

"It's our nature," Richard answered.

"You were lucky we made it this far."

She was right. Three blocks earlier the Porsche began to falter on fumes. The car's engine sputtered, having been put in neutral a block back with only enough momentum to coast to the station. As it rolled to a stop, Richard jumped out, embarrassed by the incident. The driveway attendant spotted the classic roadster before they reached the pump; he had been standing, waiting to service the vehicle even before it came to a halt. Richard grabbed the gas nozzle out of the young man's hand. Being a purist, he refused to allow anyone to touch the car. Zoey laughed at his jealous fit.

"You fill it under the license—"

"*In the rear*," he stated, cutting her off. "I know. I know. And it only takes premium leaded gas."

She smiled. Her project had been making a steady recovery. "Where should we go first, Richard? The grocery store or the department store?"

He scratched his head, not being one for shopping. His wife tried for years to get him to accompany her. Her coaxing never worked. The few times he mustered enough patience, he inevitably broke down. Stores caused him to fidget—drove him crazy. "I was thinking I might drop in on the university while you shop," he replied.

"Oh? What is the interest in the university?"

"I think it's where Frederick VonObst worked. If so, they may have information on his widow. If she's still alive, maybe they'll know how I can get in touch with her. It's a long shot but what the heck."

"Are you sure you don't want me to go along? You might have trouble again with the language barrier."

He thought about the alternative, about her accompanying him to the university or him accompanying her to stores. He grimaced shaking his head. "No, that's alright. I'm sure someone there will speak English."

"You don't want to go shopping with me?"

"Maybe. Look, Zoey, I've got this mental block against shopping. It's not you. I enjoy your company. You're a good sport and all, it's just—"

"Richard." She pointed an index finger skyward indicating she wanted him to shut up. "You need to quit while you are ahead. I understand. It is no big deal. I will come back here in two hours and pick you up. The university's main office is less than six blocks that direction," she stated, pointing north.

He smiled at her. "Zoey, you're the best. Thanks for being understanding."

"Who said I understand? It's going to cost you dearly, Captain." She winked coyly, meaning he owed her big time. Naturally, he failed to decipher her flirtatious gesture and had already scatted for the university, intent on finding more information about the mysterious professor.

The short hike to the top of the hill took him past the commanding Munster, the old church dominating the town's medieval skyline. He followed the road, Kaiser Josef Strasse, until it dead-ended into what appeared to be the admissions office. When he walked through the front door, an older woman greeted him from behind the information counter. She instantly recognized the crewcut hairstyle as military—clearly no student.

"*Sprechen Sie Englisch*? (Do you speak English?)" he asked, attempting one of the few German phrases he knew.

"Yes," she replied smiling. "You are an American. Yeah?"

"How'd you know?"

"The clothes. The hair. The air of confidence."

"That bad?" He recoiled.

She laughed out loud. "No. Actually, it is quite refreshing," she spouted, leaning forward to make sure no one could hear her next words. "These schoolchildren are such a mess. This hippie thing is way too much for me. When will they grow up?"

He wanted to laugh but thought better of it. Instead he held out his hand to shake hers. "Hello. My name is Richard O'Malley. And your name is?"

"Inga Wolfmeyer."

"Well, Inga, I think you and I are going to get along fine," he continued, holding her hand longer than necessary.

She was thrilled by his kindness and guffawed little girl fashion when he placed his second hand over theirs.

"Inga, I need help. I'm trying to locate the descendants of someone who may have worked here before the war."

"We keep all kinds of records on former employees. Was this person a teacher?"

"Yes, a professor. His name was VonObst."

"VonObst," she exclaimed.

"Why, yes. You act as though the name means something to you."

"It is because a member of our current faculty has the same last name. Her name is Lili VonObst. Professor Lili VonObst. She teaches literature."

"*Lili VonObst*." He recoiled recalling the name adjoining Frederick's on the mounting board.

"Yes."

"How old would you guess this woman is?"

"Hm-m-m. I am not too good with people's ages but if I had to venture a guess, I would say she is in her early fifties, perhaps."

He quickly surmised age fifty would put the woman in her early twenties at the time he was born. The headstone indicated Frederick was fifty-seven at time of death. It meant either she had been a much younger bride or the woman in question was a different Lili VonObst.

"Are you alright, Richard?"

"I'm sorry, Inga. I was lost in thought. Let me ask you something. Is this woman teaching here today?"

"No. This is our summer break. She will be back in two weeks, however."

"Two weeks. Inga, I can't wait two weeks. Is there any way you can give me her home address?"

"I am not supposed to give out faculty information. It is private, you know. Against the rules."

He frowned, realizing to press the issue any further would only prove pointless. Maybe he could get the address out of a phone book. As he began to walk away, she called him back.

"Richard, wait. Don't leave. I am not finished." She scrawled an address on a slip of paper. Cautiously looking both directions, she slipped the paper into his pocket. "You seem to be a nice young man. I trust you. If anyone asks, you did not get this from me," she whispered, squeezing his hand. "Good luck on your search."

He thanked her and kissed her on the cheek.

After Richard left campus, he checked the note. Inga had written *16 Milchstrasse* on the paper along with a hasty smiley face at the top, no doubt to add to her good luck wish. He asked a passerby in Pidgin German for directions. The young man, a foreign exchange student, waited for him to conclude the farcical hand signals before responding in perfect English how to get there.

The professor's home sat only a half kilometer west. He found it in less than ten minutes. Its distinctive Bavarian-styled architecture loomed picturesque on a hill by the edge of town. He eyed the front door for another ten minutes, nervously pacing the sidewalk while deliberating whether or not to ring the doorbell. He had a list of questions. And what would he say to her? Excuse me, could you possibly be my long-lost mother? Did you by chance abandon your child years ago after the war? Well, here he is. *Her-r-r-re's Richard.* And the more he thought about his situation, the more futile it seemed. Unrealistic, he told himself. Why bother? The whole idea was stupid. What were the odds it would be her?

About the time he resigned himself to return to Zoey, a small dachshund pawed his leg, begging for attention. It was a friendly pup whimpering for affection. He kneeled to pet it.

"He likes you," a woman remarked, exhausted from climbing the hill.

"He sure does," he responded, realizing the woman spoke English. How did she know? He gazed back at her while still stroking the dog's head.

"You must be an American?" She quipped.

"Yes I am. 'Must be tattooed on my forehead. You are the second person today to recognize it."

She laughed. He liked the way she easily gave into humor. He especially liked her ease with a complete stranger. And she wore an expressive face, a kind gentle face with a warm generous bearing.

"It is quite obvious you are an American. From the dialect,

I would say you were from the Midwest—Illinois or Iowa."

"Very good. It's Iowa."

"I thought so," she replied, wrinkling her face, a little puzzled. "Are you lost?"

He nodded. *"For some time."*

She looked at his eyes. His face seemed familiar. She shivered. "It is chilly out here. Would you care to come inside and join me for tea?"

"Tea?" He asked. "I thought tea was only a British custom?"

"Heavens no, young man. *It is my custom*," she replied proudly. "My name is Lili VonObst. This is Oscar," she said, motioning to the dog-friend.

"Please to meet you. Mine is Richard O'Malley," he stated, shaking the dog's paw and, then, shaking hers.

He noticed for the first time she was carrying a sack of groceries. He offered to carry it. She smiled, appearing grateful.

"Why thank you. After half a kilometer uphill it becomes quite a telling weight," she said, pausing to look at him again. "Your mother obviously taught you manners. Tell her I appreciate her hard work."

"She's a wonderful woman. I'll pass on the compliment."

Lili shuffled to the front steps, searching for the keys in her purse. After a minute of fumbling, she unlocked the door. "You are a fortunate young man. Good mothers are hard to come by. Yeah?"

"Yes. I've been very fortunate."

He held the door open. The dog scooted in first. She followed, limping past the threshold. She appeared to be in discomfort.

"Let me start the tea, Richard. How do you take yours?"

"Straight. Nothing in it."

"Not me. I love tea too much to drink it without anything. Always have. I have to add cream and sugar. It is not the same without cream and sugar."

She took the groceries from him and moved into the kitchen. He remained in the living room.

"And what brings you to the hamlet of Freiburg?" She yelled from the kitchen.

"You really want to know?" He hollered back.

"Yes. By all means. We don't get too many Americans here. This gives me a wonderful opportunity to practice my English. So, why are you here?"

He thought a few seconds on how best to answer her question—direct approach or indirect? Was she ready for what he wanted to divulge? Was she even the right person? And if she was, did it necessarily mean she was his mother? He opted for the indirect. "I'm on a journey."

"Sounds cryptic. What kind of journey?"

Again, he didn't respond at first, but thought carefully about the answer. He strolled to the grand piano sitting in the corner of the living room. An item caught his eye. On top was an old photograph of a man in his early fifties. He picked it up and blew dust off its edges. He studied the picture at length, losing track of time.

"That one is my favorite," she whispered, peering over his shoulder. "He is my deceased husband, Freddy."

"Oh, I'm sorry. You must think I'm a real snoop or something."

"Not at all. It is quite all right," she replied, stealing the picture from him and studying the photo. "He was handsome. Yes?"

"Yes. He looks so—"

"Impish." She giggled.

"No, I was going to say I thought he looked like a learned man—scholarly and wise."

"He was." She paused. "But also impetuously impish." She pressed the frame against her breast and deftly placed it back on the piano. "You know, I have not looked at this photo in years."

"Why's that?"

"Why? Ah, good question. Because he is here with me all the time," she said, pointing to her head. "And in here," she added, pointing this time to her heart. "He may be dead but his spirit has never left my side."

"How long has it been?" He asked, already knowing the answer.

"Twenty-three years."

"You must have been very young at the time."

"Indeed. We were considered an odd couple in those days. I was his student at the university. He was much older but I fell madly in love with him. Everyone said he was a confirmed bachelor but I proved them all wrong. We married four months after we met. Unfortunately, he had two brides—me and Germany. Germany won," she stated matter-of-factly, shrugging her shoulders. "Enough about me. What brings you here on this *journey* of yours?"

She motioned for him to sit on the couch with the ornate flower tapestry. Photos of Freddy scattered across two small tables at each end of the couch. As he moved to the sofa, he checked out the rest of the room. It finally dawned on him how the entire place had been stacked with Freddy's pictures—in every nook, on every shelf, table, and dresser top, anywhere pictures could prop. He smiled uneasily at the sights, these shrines to Freddy. He eventually sat. She positioned herself opposite him in a small uncomfortable looking ladder-back chair.

"I hope you don't mind us sitting. My hip gives me trouble sometimes after climbing the hill. The only thing providing me relief is resting for a few minutes in this stiff chair."

"No, problem. I've been on my feet all morning myself." He politely smiled, doing his best to guard against pent-up emotions, fearing he might reveal too much, too fast.

In spite of her relaxed deportment, he still didn't feel comfortable answering her earlier question. How could he? He felt his heart leaping from his chest. What if he slipped and said too much? He looked nervously away and back at the photograph on the piano. Maybe the butterfly box had nothing to do with his identity at all. Maybe he was pinning all hopes on something with no significance. And if it was truly her, if she really was his mother, maybe she didn't want him back in her life. Unsure, he decided to fish for answers.

"So did you and Freddy ever have any children?" His voice cracked.

She drew a slightly sickened look on her face. Her lips puckered. She frowned shaking her head. "No," she said. "*We had no son.*"

The answer devastated him. He had hoped she would have said something else like she had lost her boy years earlier; how they had been separated in a horrible accident or storm and how she searched for months and couldn't find him. He would have willingly accepted any answer, but not the one when she said, we had no son. And he was prepared to give her the benefit of every doubt he had ever harbored. He imagined many plausible explanations over the years, a variety of reasons why a three-year-old child could be cast out by his mother. He was even prepared to give her his unconditional love—the kind only a son can offer. But no confession would be forthcoming today. It had all been a mistake. What to do now?

"I just remembered, Lili," he said. "I have to be somewhere."

"What? You cannot wait for tea, Richard? I thought we could get to know each other."

"No. I wish I could, Lili." As he said the words he slithered toward the front door. "I can't. I'm sorry."

He motioned for her to remain sitting. He would see himself out. The dachshund leaped at him, again. This time he ignored the animal before shutting the door, never looking back.

(2000)

O'Keefe's packed tight with humanity. Mitchell arrived earlier than expected and settled onto a stool midway along the bar's thirty-foot course. Popping free Cajun-flavored corn munchies, he shouted out an order, a frozen strawberry margarita, to the ancient gentleman tending bar; he immediately received the stares of other patrons. "To hell with you all," he mumbled. So what if he loved *foo-foo* drinks. He was a manly man. Who cared what they thought.

He noticed an attractive blond at the end of the counter flirtatiously winking at him. She was shapely and well-endowed—*obnoxiously well-endowed*. He liked her hair—obviously a wig to make her more Dolly Parton-ish—a *sleazy* Dolly Parton. She reminded him of the type of woman his mother had always told him to avoid. Under an arm she clutched a scrawny dog. The dog resembled a bow-headed dachshund desperate for a good meal. The poor thing stared at him like a long-lost friend or a six-foot tall T-bone. Either way, he didn't feel comfortable with the eye contact from the woman or the beast. A horrible thought occurred to him. Maybe a bit of munchie got stuck between his teeth. He took the flamingo swizzle stick out of the drink the bartender had plunked down and used it to pry between the wide gap in his front teeth. Suddenly the stick broke, half of it wedged between his front incisors as a two-inch pink stem harpooned from his mouth. He couldn't get it out. He grabbed another stick from the bar inventory and attempted to pry it loose. The second stick snapped in the process, flying across the room and barely missing the bartender's head. The old-timer ducked in the nick of time. He was preparing to leave for the men's room when a diamond-encrusted set of fingers passed him dental floss.

"Here, sweetheart," she interrupted. "That's why I always carry floss. Never know when a swizzle stick's going to attack one's mouth. Happens all the time." She had apparently watched his Inspector Clouseau-like antics from afar. Her sympathy was more than he could handle. He sawed the floss through the incisors and within seconds the stick ejected. "Well, how do you feel now, lovie?" She asked.

"Like I've been rescued by the jaws of life," he retorted.

"Oh, a clever one. I like clever men. Mind if I have a seat?"

"Be my guest. Mitchell Jameson's the name," he replied, holding out his hand. "I couldn't help but notice you across the bar. Thanks for the help."

She shook his hand, noticing a wedding band.

"Oh, damn."

"What's wrong?"

"That," she said, pointing to the ring. "Why are all the cute ones always taken?"

He didn't know quite what to say. It had been a while since he had been hit on—refreshing to think he still possessed the 'old Texas charm.' He smiled. "I'll take your remark as a compliment. Can I buy you a drink? Would Godzilla, here, enjoy a few munchies?"

"How nice. Fritz is on a diet. As for me, I can always use a stiff one."

"*A stiff one?*"

"Yes, sweetheart," she replied, grabbing his crotch and holding it firmly. "I just love *stiff* things," she added, licking her lips.

He swallowed hard. A bead of sweat broke out on his forehead.

"Mitchell. There you are. I'm glad you showed up." The voice interrupting the courtship belonged to Laura Blumenthal. She patted Mitchell on the shoulder, eyeing the blonde's grip. "I see you've met Ralph."

"*Ralph?*" He asked, his voice raising an octave.

"Yes, Ralph," the blond interjected, puckering her lips.

Laura leaned over and whispered in Ralph's ear. Mitchell overheard her words. "Ralph, he's a *hetero*. Married with two little girls. He's my guest here. <u>Back off</u>."

Ralph exhaled frowning. "How the hell was I supposed to know, Laura?" His voice lowered an octave. "The man ordered a frozen strawberry margarita for crying out loud."

"Hey, wait a frigging minute, pal," Mitchell spouted, yanking Ralph's hand away. "I'll have you know lots of men drink frozen strawberry margaritas—*real men.*"

"The only ones I know are queer," Ralph countered, disappointed by the revelation. "Cock tease."

Mitchell's mouth fell open. He turned to Laura. "I've been called a lot of things in my life. That's a first."

Ralph moved back to the bar stool on the far side of the bar, carrying his little friend under an arm. Fritz yelped, whining for a crack at a munchie. Mitchell tossed the dog a morsel when Ralph wasn't looking. The canine easily caught it, trapping it in its shallow snout and swallowing it whole.

"Well, at least you made one new friend tonight," Laura teased. She abruptly turned and hollered for "the usual" to the bartender, in this case meaning her standard margarita on the rocks with salt, shaken not blended. The grandfatherly fellow didn't hear her request—the hearing aid had been conveniently turned off. Next, she stood on the stool hailing him with a shrill whistle. He spotted her and signaled he would have her drink ready "in a jiff." "Mitchell, did you order any food from Stephan. He makes the best bratwurst sandwiches, you know."

"No, I did not know his specialty" he responded, still miffed with Ralph. "*I'm not clairvoyant.*"

She ignored Mitchell's comment and ordered them each a sandwich. She was right. The sandwiches were unforgettable. He consumed his in three huge bites.

Neither one spoke for some time. He mostly watched and listened. Patrons of the establishment, all Dr. Laura patients at one time or another, dropped by her barstool-office to pay a visit and a crack at free advice. Mitchell quietly sat and observed the procession of lovelorn clientele line up to bug her with personal questions. Her Godfather-like status amused him. The bowing, hugging, and kissy-face antics almost seemed scripted. He thought she should be renamed Guido or Vito, deciding it would only piss her off; he certainly didn't need to antagonize her any more than necessary. He was also amazed at how *normal* her clients appeared. If there were 'queers' among those seeking free counseling, he never would have guessed. Most of the folks appeared like stereotypical neighbors back in Austin—average and boring. The entire scene shattered any preconceived ideas he had how homosexuals should look. And after forty-five minutes and a third margarita, Laura finally had a chance to chat with him again.

"What do you think, Mitchell?" She asked, eyeing the last of her departing clientele.

"The fans? The Laura Blumenthal faithful, you mean?"

"Yes."

He thought for a few seconds how best to respond—*tactfully*. "Well, they sure had me fooled."

"*What do you mean by that*?" She asked, straight-faced serious.

"Oh, nothing. Forget it."

"No. I want to hear what you have to say. Get the hostility out in the open."

"Okay, since you insist," he replied, a little annoyed. "If all those folks are your clients, it means they're all—"

"Gays?"

"Right. *Gays*. Frankly, they fooled me. I mean, I had this image they'd all be tough coach-looking woman with butchy haircuts. And the guys—the guys I figured to be running around in leotards. You know, the proverbial *flaming* image and, I suppose, the screwy thinking you'd probably expect coming from me," he answered, downing the last of his drink. "But they weren't."

"Disappointed?"

"Not really. Confused a bit—*definitely not disappointed*. Believe me."

"It appears what you're saying is over time you conjured a preconceived image, an delusion if you will, of how you *think* homosexuals should look."

"Guess so. Don't we all? I mean, when I walked in your office, didn't you have some preconceptions of how a writer should look, talk, act like?"

"Sure."

"There you go."

"So you think as humans we tend to create falsehoods to facilitate what we don't understand?"

"Falsehoods might be a little strong. Let's call 'em illusions. If it wasn't for illusions, how would we make it through the day to cope with life's ugly truths?"

"I'm glad you understand, Mitchell," she responded, pausing to reposition herself on the barstool. She turned to face him head-on. "Tell me all about your new book. We've never discussed it."

"You don't really want to know."

"Sure I do. I want to hear all the *ugly truths*."

He laughed uneasily. "I can't tell you every detail," he said, lowering his voice to a whisper. "It's bad luck, you know," he added with a wink.

"Fine. Just share the gist of it."

"Okay. Here it goes: It's a story of two men, two generations who have to contend with war. Their respective wars: World War II and Vietnam. They're separated in time but not in spirit. One's the father. One's the son. One's a German. The other, an American. They have to deal with war atrocities. How they deal with their *demons* determines their fate. If they change, metamorphose, adapt to their worlds, worlds with distinct rights and wrongs, they survive. If they don't, they perish."

"Sort of like butterflies."

"Exactly. Very perceptive."

"And do they survive? Do they rid themselves of their *demons*?" She flashed finger air quotes.

"It's a secret, Laura. You'll have to read the book to find out." He smirked.

"Not fair, Mitchell." She complained, tapping her foot on the stool's truss. "Now, you've made me hyper-curious. Why did you pick this subject? This topic? It doesn't seem to follow your past genres."

"I thought you said you hadn't read my stuff?"

"I hadn't until I met you. You sparked my interest. I completed your fourth book late last night. You've got quite a talent."

"Thanks."

"So back to my original question. Why this subject matter? Why those two men?"

"Shouldn't this sort of thing be left to our sessions?"

"Believe me, it'll come up again," she said, grinning. "Think of it as double-billing. Tonight, however, it's only gonna cost you a margarita."

She waved her empty glass in his face. He hollered at Stephen for a refill.

"For now, Laura, let's just say I picked that particular subject because I can relate to the two men—we're kindred souls separated by time and space. Each of us has to change or we lose it all. And, of course, there's the other reason."

"And what, pray tell, might that be?" She asked.

"It's been twenty-eight years, Laura, and I'm right on schedule."

SIX
(1945)

The supply truck arrived early in the morning as Frederick had predicted. It backed tight against the loading dock where the boys could sneak under the tarp draped over its cargo bed and stow undetected by passing sentries. Frederick provided both the lookout and go-ahead signal. With each coast-is-clear nod, another boy-soldier scrambled into the truck's bed, clearing room for the next stowaway who also hid among boxes and crates. The tarp, painted with bright red crosses on its sides, kept human freight from being exposed. No one would dare look inside because international relief vehicles were off limits.

The meager supplies of blankets and medicine for Stalag 4 unloaded all too quickly while the last batch of boy-soldiers scrambled inside before the truck could pull away. The driver, a neutral observer from Switzerland, had been kept distracted by Stefan until everyone boarded. Fortunately, with the camp embroiled in pandemonium (in anticipation of arriving British liberation forces), the standard exit inspection at Checkpoint C was undermanned. The lone sentry waved the driver through the gate without once looking up. Ignorant of his cargo or why his truck seemed unusually sluggish climbing the steep grade out of Bremen Valley, the driver remained intent tackling the road. The ascent proved slothful at best, slowed by debris scattered across the narrow roadway. The highway littered with abandoned trucks and armored vehicles out of gas, petrol being a rare commodity in Germany's dog days. But the driver maneuvered through the carnage, slaloming back and forth until he overtook the crest of the hill three kilometers from the prison. When he reached a wooded area near the lake, he upshifted. The truck jerked backward, the movement catching the passengers off guard. Two of the boys fell crashing against crates. The disturbance made little difference to the stowaways. This was the spot where they would disembark. They would hide in the forest until the British secured the valley. Once the British arrived, they would surrender and begin the long trek home.

Frederick opened the rear flap. From the vantage on the back of the truck, they had a commanding view of the valley and the idle smokestacks in the distance. Frederick gave his squad another go-ahead signal, this time to jump out; one-by-one they leaped from the rig and dashed into the protective camouflage of the nearby forest. When they were sufficiently far from the road, Frederick gathered them in a tight circle and instructed them to count off to make sure all had made it safely.

"Do you think they will discover we are missing, Freddy?" Stefan asked, panting heavily from the ordeal.

"They probably already have," Frederick replied, matter-of-factly.

"Do you think they will be coming after us right away?" One of the youth fussed.

"No. Never. They cannot spare the manpower. We are safe for now."

Given Freddy's assurances, the band of runaways felt good about their chances. They hiked under a canopy of trees, crisscrossing worn hiking trails that took them deep into the belly of the forest. Rumblings of faraway artillery bombardments provided an eerie escort. Even in the pristine environs of the woods, shell explosions reminded them of an ongoing war. They were, after all, surrounded by conflict and caught in the crosshair of both an unseen enemy and a potential firing squad. Frederick suggested the boys sing, hoping their voices would drown the nerve-racking explosions. The small repertoire sang traditional German folk songs and sounded divine in the open-air cathedral.

In one respect they were fortunate. It was a beautiful spring day. May foliage bloomed spectacularly with wildflowers carpeted everywhere and boldly contrasting fields of human carnage less than ten kilometers away. With it being unusually warm, a few of the boys shed their uniforms, discarding jackets on the ground and tossing swastikas and German crosses into mounds of dandelions and violets. Stefan suggested the rest of them wear white armbands in case they stumbled onto the enemy. By the time they reached the lake, the crew resembled more a Boy Scout patrol than a pack of war-weary deserters.

Like most hastily prepared plans, theirs had flaws with the most obvious being not enough food. When they set out, Frederick had no idea how many days would be needed to hide in the forest. Other than the duffel bag packed with Stefan's bratwurst sandwiches and a few cooking utensils, each lad had been ordered to bring his own food stashed in his own backpack. Unfortunately, Sergeant Freddy never had time to inspect their gear. Most of his soldiers were lousy planners and exhausted their personal rations by the second day, forcing everyone to scavenge the woods for wild game and berries. Frederick's entomology background helped the situation. He identified the natural foodstuffs of the forest—mushrooms, tree roots, and varied species of beetles—for a stew concoction appropriately labeled "Freddy's borscht." Everyone hated the borscht except Freddy. Boiling water became necessary as the canteens quickly exhausted. It meant fires needed to be lit and regulated, keeping smoke to a minimum for fear of giving their position away.

On the third night three of the boys developed diarrhea and dehydration. Earlier in the day Frederick had identified a medicinal plant which could relieve the cramping the boys were experiencing. With a handful of healthy youth and a solitary flashlight, he set out to find the herb, this as storm clouds rolled in. For two nights they'd experienced perfect dry weather. Not this night. A cold front pushed through and with it a steady drizzle. To add to the woes, they had nothing to repel the rain—no tents or rain gear. The unusually balmy temperature plunged with the passage of the front. Everyone got miserably cold, especially those already sick. No one wanted to sing. No one felt like doing much except huddling for warmth. The euphoric atmosphere of days earlier gave way to despair.

After the detail left to find medicinal plants, Stefan was left in charge and told to boil water and make sure the infirm soldiers were given plenty of liquid. The fire would keep them warm through the night. It would be their first nighttime campfire, an exception to Frederick's prohibition to evening fires.

Shortly after the scouting patrol found the plants, the flashlight's batteries failed. It took a combination of dead reckoning and blind luck to find the way back to camp. A half kilometer away they smelled the smoke from the burning campfire; less than a quarter kilometer from camp they saw the flames and used the blaze as a homing beacon. The modest bivouac had been converted into a raging bonfire.

"Thank God you made it, Freddy," Stefan yelled, the first to spot the weary scouting party. "We all thought you had been captured or lost. We stoked the fire hoping you'd see it and find your way back." Stefan hugged his leader. "I guess it worked. Yeah?"

Frederick voiced displeasure. "Damn it all, Stefan. Can't you ever follow orders?" He snapped.

"But I thought—"

"That's your problem," Frederick interrupted. "You think too much. You don't follow orders." He poked the old one in the temple.

"But—"

"I specifically told you *no large fires*. Now we'll need to move everyone first thing in the morning. We've been spotted for sure, either by the enemy or our own troops."

No one said anything after the outburst. Frederick's anger, spawned by days of anxiety, proved too much for the old man. Stefan slunk to the lake's beachfront, distraught he had failed his closest friend once again. He spent the rest of the night alone, curled up under a fallen tree and getting soaked by a relentless drizzle.

Early the next morning, the cold front gave way to sparkling clear skies; the winds had ceased altogether. The smoke from the smoldering campfire soared vertically, pinpointing their location. By the time Frederick awoke and smothered the embers, the black plume had already led the German patrol to the spot. Even before any of the deserters stirred, they had been completely surrounded.

"Well. Well. What have we here?" The lieutenant mocked, waving his Luger pistol in their faces. "We have stumbled upon unarmed little boys and an old man who no longer want to play war." He spouted. His comrades laughed. They cocked their rifles, taking close aim on each of the youth. "Could it be the group of deserters from Bergen-Belsen? Well, Sergeant, are you?"

Frederick swallowed hard, refusing to answer. The lieutenant cocked the Luger and placed its barrel in the mouth of a sickly boy. "I am waiting for an answer, Sergeant. Do not make me wait much longer or this one dies."

Thoughts of Lili and their infant son flashed through Frederick's mind. How sweet their lives could have been had he remained in Freiburg. How simple their existence. But, no, he chose a far different path and, now, a child was going to be murdered in cold blood by a nameless executioner and he blamed himself. "Yes. We are the ones," he finally blurted.

"As I thought," the lieutenant responded, uncocking the gun, placing it back in its holster. "I don't know what you did, but you enraged your commandant when you deserted. He put a hefty price on all your heads. There are patrols like ours everywhere scouring the area looking for you. Fortunately, he wants you kept alive. If it were up to me, I would shoot you here, right now, and be done with it, you damned coward." He spit in Frederick's face.

"Listen," Frederick pleaded. "These boys are mere children. They should never have been involved in this war in the first place. Let them go. I have money. Lots of it. How much is each child worth to you?"

"More than you can afford old man."

"But I have British pounds back in Freiburg. Lots."

"Freiburg? British pounds?" the man sneered. "Hell, we are being paid in *gold*. The more of your boy-soldiers we bring back, the more gold we make."

"But I am the one the commandant really wants. I am worth more than all of them combined."

"And why is that?"

"Because I made it personal. I abandoned him. We are good friends, you know. Do you not see? I let him down."

"You, a lowly sergeant, *friends* with Heinrich Goerne?" The man laughed hysterically. "Now I know you are a liar. The esteemed doctor has no friends."

The lieutenant shoved Frederick to the ground, frisking him and searching pockets. At the same time, the other bounty hunters frisked the deserters, yanking the white armbands off their sleeves and smacking a few in the face. They marched the squad out of the forest and along the road to Bergen-Belsen with Sergeant Freddy taking up the rear.

Stefan watched the arrest from behind the fallen tree near the beach, powerless to help. Stealthily, he chased after the procession making sure not to be seen, ducking behind bushes and shrubs as he pursued. He followed the entourage as long as he could but within an hour the patrol had marched back inside Stalag 4's third fence and Section A. Except for a handful of guards and endless piles of stacked corpses, the only ones remaining in the abandoned prison were the bounty hunters, Frederick's band of boy-soldiers, and, of course, Doctor Death.

(1972)

Zoey astutely figured out Richard had suffered a bad afternoon. The first sign—his lack of interest in driving the Porsche. She chauffeured them home. The second worrisome signal—his refusal to discuss Lili VonObst. Even the short ride to the cottage felt awkward and seemed to last forever. Richard's behavior, markedly different from the exuberance a few hours earlier, had her concerned, again, for his mental health. And now he refused to talk at all.

When they got back to the cottage, he said he wanted to go for a walk by himself in the meadow. She said she would prepare dinner while he was gone and how it would be ready when he returned. Don't push him further away, she told herself. Give him space.

Near dusk he walked back through the door. Everything had been prepared awaiting his return, as she said—an elaborate spread intended to take his mind off worries. Sitting opposite him, she studied his eyes. He appeared less troubled and more relaxed.

"You look better now, Richard."

"What do you mean by that?" He asked.

"Nothing. Nothing at all. All I meant was—"

"I'm being creepy again? Is that it?" He snapped.

"No. Not at all Richard. I am just concerned about you."

She placed her hand over his. He immediately pulled away.

"I don't need your concern, Zoey. Maybe your prayers but definitely not your concern."

"Prayers? Whatever do you mean?"

"I mean, I've made my mind up. I'm leaving for Stuttgart

tomorrow. I'm going to serve out my tour in Vietnam like a good obedient soldier."

"But why, Richard? I thought you hated it?"

"Look, Zoey, I appreciate your *concern*s for me. I appreciate everything you've tried to do for me but I have absolutely nothing going on in my life right now. There's no reason for me not to go. Besides, I don't know who the hell I am right now. I thought I'd discover myself but I didn't."

He looked away. She tried placing her hand back over his. "Richard, talk to me. Look at me. Have you not figured out by now I am your friend? That I care about you?"

"You have been a real friend, Zoey. A real trooper. I don't know what I would have done without you."

"Then, talk to me Richard. Tell me what happened this afternoon."

He groaned, deciding to give in to Zoey and permit her to listen to his problems one more time. "I found her," he finally stated.

"Lili VonObst?"

"Yes."

"Did you talk with her?"

"Oh, yes."

"Is she your mother?"

He shook his head 'No.'

Zoey seized his hand. "I am sorry it did not work out."

"It's okay. It was just a crazy notion of mine all these years to find my real parents and why they abandoned me. That's all."

"I don't think it is crazy at all."

He smiled uneasily. "Perhaps, you are right, Zoey, but it is time for me to leave. Life isn't a make-believe fantasy world tucked neatly away in a cottage in the Black Forest. Life is harsh and cruel. My reality is I'm a soldier. I am what I am. I'm not your *project* any longer. I'm a career officer in the U.S. Army and duty calls. Who am I to question orders? To question destiny?"

She didn't plead with him again. She knew his mind had been made up. Any attempt to change it would prove futile. And they did not speak after dinner. Later at night, however, she cried herself to sleep. The open air ceiling could not conceal her emotions. He lay in bed and listened to her sobbing, realizing for the first time the depth of her emotional commitment to him.

It was 2:00 a.m. when he awoke to the sounds of wheezing, her needful gasps for breath. For minutes he listened to the asthma attack hoping it would subside; the fit quickly deteriorated into a gurgling seizure ceasing all at once. The abrupt silence gave him an uneasy chill and he dashed to her bedside hoping she had simply rolled over and gone back to sleep. Instead, he found her unconscious and sprawled prostrate on the floor. Her eyes stared void of life. Her cotton night shirt drenched in perspiration and clung to her body, clammy to the touch. *She had stopped breathing.* Instinctively, he tilted her head back, fingering out mucus choking her ability to inhale. He began mouth-to-mouth resuscitation, exhaling into her collapsed lungs. Less than a minute later, she was breathing on her own. He carried her into the bathroom and propped her against the shower stall wall, and opened the valve on the hot water. Soon, steam loosened her constricted lungs; her measured breaths becoming less deliberate, less forced. She began to breathe normally. He watched her face turn from blue to the pale white hue of her natural coloring.

After minutes of recuperating, the steam began to cloud the cramped bathroom with mist, completely enshrouding her shivering body. Water vapor dripped off her nose and face and mixed with her tears, pooling in the shower's basin. He watched the mixture swirl into the drain and shuddered at the thought he may have caused this attack. And he felt ashamed.

"Zoey, I'm sorry I upset you."

She said nothing but simply watched his eyes. Seconds later, she reached out and touched his cheek. Her soaked nightshirt now revealed her naked body and the subtle erect nipples. She posed magnificently beautiful.

"Richard," she whispered, "Please don't leave me. I think I love you."

He kissed the palm of her hand and began to cry. "Oh, Zoey, if you only knew how much I needed to hear somebody tell me those words. It's been so long. So terribly long."

She pulled him toward her. He kissed her, wrapping his arms around her waist, and embraced her tight against his body, thrusting her back against the wall. She reciprocated, pulling herself into him. And they made love, two lovers swept in a journey nearing its end.

Late the next morning, Richard awoke to the smells of another Zoey breakfast. Even without much sleep, he felt invigorated and ready to take on the world. He climbed out of bed, still naked, and touched his toes, popping his vertebra one at a time. When he straightened up, he noticed his duffel bag in the corner of the room and the bulging outline of the shadow box pressed against canvas. He unzipped the bag and removed the heirloom, deciding to show it to Zoey, but strategically positioned it in front of his genitalia for modesty sake.

Zoey had already dressed and was standing next to the sink. Her back faced the bedroom when Richard strutted in.

"What do you think?" He asked, pointing to the butterflies.

At first she was a little startled by the sight but, abruptly began snickering. "They're beautiful," she teased. "And big."

"When you say *big*, you mean this?" He asked, lifting the box. "Or this?" He eyed the butterflies, waving the box in the air.

She laughed again. "*Both*," she correctly answered. She leapt, snatching the shadow box out of his hands. "And what is this?"

"It's what I thought linked me to my past. It's the butterfly box I told you about. See the inscription in the corner? The inscription is why I thought the VonObst's were my parents."

She inspected it more closely, amazed the butterflies were still perfectly preserved. After a few moments a thought suddenly occurred to her and she began to giggle. "Oh, my goodness. This is funny, Richard. Such a, *a coincidence*."

"Coincidence? What do you mean?"

"I mean these butterflies. Do you know what they are?"

"Sure. Yellow and black butterflies," he joked.

"No. These are a very rare variety. They are called Old World Swallowtails. They migrate only once every twenty-eight years from beyond the Jura Mountains. And guess where they migrate to?" Her eyebrows rose anticipating his answer.

"I have no idea. Where, Zoey?"

She giggled again, shaking her head in disbelief,

wondering if he would ever believe her without proof. Grabbing his hand, she tugged him out the back door. They scurried down the hill, Richard doing his best to keep up. When they reached the perfect spot in the meadow, sufficiently far from the house, she let go of his hand.

"Alright, Zoey, you've succeeded in exposing me totally naked to both God and nature. What's the big surprise?"

She raised both hands skyward and began twirling and laughing; the ribbons in her hair flew horizontal as she spun. "This is the surprise, Richard. This is the place. This is where they come. Can you not see them?"

He looked at her skeptically, not sure if she was teasing or had gone completely insane. *See them*? He wondered. See whom? He looked around the meadow and saw nothing unusual except the storm cloud approaching from the south. "I don't see anything other than rain heading our way. I'm going back inside."

As he began to walk away, she grabbed his hand, holding it firmly, preventing him from escaping.

"Look again," she said, nodding her head toward the south.

He glanced at her out of the corners of his eyes, even more bewildered but decided it best to placate her mood and play her game. He looked south one more time. The gray cloud approached faster. It began to resemble a dust cloud in appearance—swirling, pulsating, and moving erratically with energy. The sight hypnotized him. He watched it draw nearer the meadow, encircling its wooded perimeter in cyclonic formation, the gray erupting into vibrant yellow and black.

"My God. It's them, isn't it? It's the butterflies."

"Yes, Richard," she replied. "Twenty-eight years in the

making. They have been here all week. Can you believe it? It must be a good sign for us. A sign sent from heaven." She shed her clothes and abandoned them on the ground.

"What are you doing, Zoey?"

"I am getting naked, *like you*. What does it look like I am doing?"

"But—"

She pushed him on the ground. He fell flat on his back. She jumped on top of him with her legs straddling his chest, laughing all the while. "No *buts*, Richard. Remember?"

"I just thought if you wanted to make love we should climb the hill, go back inside and—"

"And what?" She interrupted. "Look around. Days like this come but once in a lifetime. Make love to me out here in the open with butterflies swirling around our bodies. Think you can handle it, *Hansel*?"

He grinned, pulling her toward him. "You'd better believe it, *Gretel*. You'd better believe it."

(2000)

"How's it hanging this week, buddy boy?" The voice rattled the speakerphone speaker.

"Great. I'm glad you called, Harvey. I'm almost finished with the book."

"Outstanding. When do I get the first draft?"

"In a week."

"That's phenomenal, Mitchell. I can't believe it. This is absolutely wonderful. So, tell me. I'm *dying* to know. What happens to the two guys who go off to war? Do they bite the dust hideously or heroically?"

"Why would you ask?"

"Because *all* your main characters die. You write tragedies. Tragedy is your trademark."

"No, I don't *and it's not my trademark.*"

"Hey, I'm not complaining. Tragedy sells. It's what we want—books that sell. We want readers to bawl like babies. I've always said sentimental emotion is good for the pocketbook."

"Wow. I never really thought about it that way," Mitchell moaned.

"Look, I know you've been through a lot the past month. To be able to write this thing, deal with the separation, get counseling, *and* reconcile with Susan. It's all pretty incredible if you ask me."

Mitchell Jameson didn't know exactly how to respond to his agent's words of admiration. While the book did, indeed, near completion, he was not as confident his personal problems would reach the same finality.

"All I meant is I'm sure Susan will be pleased you're finally coming home."

Again, Mitchell said nothing.

"You are going back to Susan when you're finished, aren't you?" Harvey persisted.

"Not right away. I've still got issues to work out with my counselor."

"Listen, Mitchell, psychotherapy, counseling, personal guidance, whatever the hell you want to call it nowadays, it's not a panacea for every ill. Take it from someone who knows."

"I thought you said it helped your marriage?"

"It did. But it also doesn't mean diddley squat if your heart's not in it or if you haven't made a commitment to making the marriage work. It boils down to you wanting it. All the counseling in the world isn't going to make you desire the other person again. It's not going to make you forgive them or yourself for mistakes made. That has to come from within. Make sense?"

"Yes, and it's scary advice coming from you."

"Hey, the Klanowitz family has a long proud tradition. Not a single divorce in over eight generations."

"Pretty impressive, Harvey."

"You're telling me. Also makes you think twice before reneging on your marriage vows. Once you do that, it sets a family precedent. *Capisce?*"

"Yeah, I understand. In fact, I'm thoroughly amazed. This is a side of you I didn't know existed."

They both laughed.

"Just keep this in mind, Mitchell: Your counselor's in the business to keep you coming back through the door. The more often you pass the turnstile, the more money she makes."

"*And the more it costs you.*"

"Absolutely. I am paying the tab but it doesn't matter if it's coming out of my pocket, yours, or an insurance company's. The fact is psychologists never tell you you're healthy. They never say you don't need to see 'em any longer. *You* have to take the initiative and tell them."

"Based on what?"

"Well, there's the catch, buddy boy—you have to feel good enough to stop going. Problem with that is ninety-five percent of psychologists' patients never feel good enough. I think it's all a conspiracy. I think the bastards have ways of messing with your mind. About the time you're starting to feel good, they remind you how Uncle Milty sodomized you as a small boy."

"I didn't know your uncle abused you."

"No, no, no. I was speaking metaphorically."

"Sure you were," Mitchell chuckled. "That's why you and your uncle still go on those long fishing trips together. He can't stand the thought of leaving your behind."

"Asshole."

"Gotcha."

"Listen. Just think about everything I said. Okay?"

"Okay. Hey, Harvey, I gotta run. Someone's ringing the frigging doorbell. I think it's the electrician. See you."

"Ciao, my man."

After the fifth ring, Mitchell reached the door, annoyed by the contractor's unnerving persistence. The worker greeted him without a glance as he read the work order off a clip board. "Howdy. Says here you're having problems with the hot tub—won't turn on."

Mitchell acknowledged the problem and invited the man inside. As he spoke, the man tilted his head sideways recognizing the voice.

"My God. *It's you.* I met you the other night at the club. It's me—Ralph. Remember?"

"Oh, shit." Mitchell groaned.

"Well, isn't this a weird coinky-dink. I am actually standing on the front porch of the Mitchell Jameson residence, one of the most acclaimed authors of the modern day American novel. This is an honor, sir. Now, do me a favor. Stay right here. Have I got a surprise for you."

Ralph sprinted to the rear door of his van. He removed a small package and dashed back to Mitchell with the surprise in his hands.

"Look, Fritz. It's your friend, Mitchell."

The dog wagged its tail furiously and leaped into Mitchell's arms, licking its newest friend's face.

"That's so darned cute," Ralph remarked. "He doesn't lick face with any of my other man-friends."

A little overwhelmed by the show of affection, Mitchell tried holding the dachshund at bay but it squirmed free. "So, Ralph, you're an electrician by day and—"

"*A drag queen by night*," Ralph finished.

"Uh-huh. And you carry your dog around every—"

"Everywhere I go." Ralph giggled. "Like Mary."

"Mary?"

"You know, silly. Mary who had a little lamb. It's fleece as white as snow. It followed her to—"

"*To work one day*," Mitchell finished, deadpan.

"I see you haven't forgotten your nursery rhymes or your clever sense of humor. You tease, you."

Mitchell groaned, again. "No. I've got two little girls who recite this stuff all the time, or have you forgotten?" He asked, pointing to the wedding band.

"Right. Your little girls. I love girls, too. Bet you couldn't tell?"

"Sure had me fooled, Ralph. Well, come on in. Let me show you the hot tub."

Mitchell led Ralph through the house and out the back door

to the wooden deck supporting the Jacuzzi. From the rear of the house the yard dropped off sharply to a huge meadow. The deck projected over a steep incline and afforded a spectacular view. Wildflowers and native grasses mixed as far as the eye could see making it a rare sight for late-October in the Rockies. A thick pine and spruce forest surrounded the meadow from a nearby mountain range.

"Wow. This is absolutely beautiful. I've never seen anything like it around these parts. You must irrigate or something to get everything to grow so green," Ralph remarked, pointing to the vast meadow.

"There are a few natural springs in the area. That's why I bought the place, so I don't have to contend with environmentalists."

"Oh, don't they make your blood boil. They're nasty radical around Vail."

Ralph's comment surprised Mitchell.

"You can say that again, brother."

"Sister."

"Huh?"

"You mean, *sister*."

"Whatever. Say, would you care for a beer or something? Kinda warm today."

Ralph wrinkled his face thinking on the offer. "What the hell. It's the last job. Why not?"

Mitchell left to fetch both of them a beer, still carrying Fritz under an arm. Ralph opened the panel to the tub and began running diagnostics. By the time the beers were served, the master electrician already had the problem fixed.

"It didn't take you long, Ralph."

"Just a circuit breaker. Sometimes if you keep it continuously cycling it'll trip. No biggie." He grinned. "Happens all the time. I adjusted your timer. No charge for the visit, either."

"Why, thank you. You know, I'm a real klutz with anything electronic. I had to take a course to learn how to turn on my laptop. And if you think that's bad, I still haven't figured out my new telephone."

"Well, Mitchell, you sure know how to write."

"Thanks, Ralph, but you gave me the impression the other night you had no idea who I was."

"I didn't then. Laura told me after you left. I bought one of your books the next day. Couldn't put it down. Cried my eyes out all night because of you."

"Sorry. Which one was it, anyway?"

"My left." He giggled, pointing to his left eye. "That's a joke, Mitchell."

"I get it. What I meant was which—"

"Which *book* did I read? I know. I know. It was the one about the woman trying to find out what happened to her grandfather. Tell you what, the story seriously got to me. I mean, when I found out about the cannibals, I thought I'd have a conniption shit fit. But—"

"But what?"

"The first chapter was the toughest. Needs a little work. A little too—"

"Graphic? Violent?"

"Too gory. Too *icky*." Ralph winced, his hands flaying wildly in front of his face.

"Enough already, Ralph. You made your point. Let me ask

you something."

"Go right ahead. I'm all ears, Mitchell."

Ralph sat on the edge of the deck. Mitchell sat opposite.

"Well, it's like this: Sometimes I get a little criticism because my stories don't always look at things from a female perspective. I mean, there is either not enough heroines or not enough romance. You know?"

"Sex for the gander."

"Exactly. They're good stories with good wholesome messages but—"

"They don't pull in big enough cross-sections of readers because they don't suck up to what the publishers are screaming for. Right? They don't degrade to the lowest common denominator?"

"*Right.*"

"Well, here's what I think, Mitchell: You can't please all the people all the time. Old-timers want their storybook heroes to be over seventy. Wives want their heroes to behave the way their husbands once did when they were first courting. Heterosexual men want raunchy sex. Cowboys like to read about cowboys. Indians like to read about Indians. Everybody has their own likes and dislikes. Fact is you can't please everybody with every story. The best you can do is to write from the heart, Mitchell Jameson's heart." He poked Mitchell in the chest. "You gotta stay true to yourself. If you do that and tell a good story, it will always sell."

Mitchell nodded his head. "Good advice, Ralph."

"Why thank you. Now, tell me. How's the next bestseller coming?"

"Pretty good. I think. I've been following your formula. I

just haven't decided exactly how to end it. There are some things I don't fully know, yet."

"You mean haven't created, yet."

"No, I wouldn't use the term *created*. This story goes a little deeper. It's more . . . *personal*. Maybe you can help me out with the ending. I could use a—"

"*A woman's perspective.*"

"Uh-h-h-h. Yeah? Something along those lines," Mitchell replied. "Did anyone ever tell you how you have an annoying habit of inter—"

"Interrupting?"

"Yeah."

Ralph grinned sheepishly. "Nope. Never. But as far as your ending goes, I think the best stories have happy endings."

"For instance?"

"Fairy-tales. You know, *they lived happily ever after*. Can your story have an ending like that?"

Mitchell thought over the suggestion before answering.

"Only if it really happens, Ralph," he replied. "Only if it happens."

SEVEN
(1945)

"Welcome to my hell, Sergeant VonObst."

Heinrich opened his arms, stretching them wide in a feigned display of sincerity. It was his way of signifying how everything within sight belonged to him. 'Welcome to *my* world, the secretive world of Section A,' would have been more apropos, for he had always wanted Frederick to see what he had committed his life's work to the past five years—*the exterminations.* So, he smiled grimly and pivoted his body sideways to expose the stacked corpses, allowing the captured squad of deserters a better view.

"You finally get to see the *ugly truth,* Frederick. It is a shame, you know. I had hoped we could have been friends after the war. Good friends. But, now, that is impossible. Yes? Now everyone will know about our solution here. *Our final solution.* All because a bomb accidentally dropped on our cleansing factory—one errant bomb. Such a tragedy. Once the furnaces were destroyed, so was our ability to burn bodies and conceal the evidence. We were forced to start piling them here in the open." He suddenly yelled, shaking his fists at the corpses, "Damned you." He reached in a pocket and pulled out a handkerchief, smothering it over his nose and mouth. "The smell isn't as bad as it could have been had there been food in their bellies. With a little luck, perhaps, the ravens will pick at their bones and clean things up."

Frederick felt his knees buckle, stunned by the sight. One of the boys collapsed and began to vomit. The others began to cry or look away.

"Commandant," Frederick pleaded. "Please let these children go home. They should not be exposed to such things and—"

"It is *Heinrich*," he interrupted. "We can dispense with formalities, here. After all, are we not friends? We should stick together. Yeah?"

"Alright, Heinrich. Whatever you say. Whatever you want. If you will only let the boys go. Please. I take full responsibility. They were under my command. They would not have left here without me. I am the one who deserted."

"Deserted? Not you. You were merely leading your band of boy scouts out of hell. Do you realistically think that is desertion? Do you think I could blame you for escaping hell?" He asked, becoming more reflective. "No, my friend. On the contrary. I admire you even more. It shows you have the courage of your convictions, but it is too late for apologies. Today is a day of reckoning for us all. You see, Germany has surrendered. Did you know we surrendered?"

"No, I did not."

"Of course not. You were hiding in the forest. How could you know such news?" He replied. "It happened late yesterday afternoon. That is why I paid these gentlemen to find you. I knew you would want to hear the good news and share in the joy with me, like old times. Two close friends sharing things. I will bet you are looking forward to returning home to Lili. Yeah?"

"Very much. I should never have left her in the first place."

"*Should never have left her?*" Heinrich laughed. "Frederick, men like you and me, we never change. That is our nature. We love the wrong things in life. Why, if you were given the chance to do it over again, to fight this war, you would. You would not think twice about it," he mocked, shaking his head. "But the sad truth is you probably do not have a clue what I am saying, do you?"

"A clue? I know this much, Heinrich. You're insane."

"As are you for leaving your heaven in Freiburg to come to hell."

Heinrich dismissed the guards. At the same time he took out a sidearm, pointing it at the boys. He ordered the remaining SS executioner to bring out the last batch of Jewish inmates—twenty naked starving children all under the age of twelve.

"We have been quite busy here, Frederick. *Quotas. Quotas. Quotas.* I'm tired of Gestapo quotas. Fifty thousand to dispose of in less than seven days. Far too many. You see, Hemler and I had a bet. I said it could be done. He said it could not. He lost. He was supposed to blow his brains out." He giggled. "He was always a poor loser, you know."

Frederick kept his mouth shut. He watched the young Jews herded to a huge cylindrical tank. A solitary steel door with a peephole near its latch provided the only way in and out. Above the door a skull and crossbones had been painted with the words, "Danger. Do Not Enter." The children's heads had been shaved bald. Their naked bodies revealed the malnutrition suspected weeks earlier. Their boney cheekbones protruded from their emaciated heads; their bellies distended from days without food. And they said nothing. They neither cried nor murmured nor uttered a solitary sound. Instead, they milled anxiously in front of the door, eager to end it all. It was as though they knew their situation hopeless and welcomed death.

"They were even calmer a few days ago, Frederick, thanks to the Brodifacoum. Unfortunately, we ran out. Now look at them. They are anxious and want to go inside. They're eager to end the pain." He studied Frederick's face, recognizing the concern. "Ah, yes. I see the sight of these little ones upsets you. It upset me for a while. After all, I am a doctor. I am supposed to save lives, not take them. But I soon realized Jews are not human—*they are locusts*. They are vermin who must be eliminated if our race is to survive. If Germany is to survive." He stopped to look at Frederick. "These are the last of the prisoners at Stalag 4. I saved these for you, Frederick. That is what friends do. They share."

"But they are children, Heinrich."

"Ah-h-h, but the worst kind. They are the avengers. Kill the children, Hemler told me, and you kill the memories—*you kill retribution*."

"But you certainly cannot kill them. It is not right. You cannot."

"Me? I am not going to kill anyone, Frederick. My days of exterminating Jews are over. Now it is your turn. And your choice."

"My choice? What do you mean?"

"I mean this: I'm giving you a way out of your disgrace. Out of your desertion and the predicament you put yourself in when you abandoned this post and left me alone. And here is your option: Either kill the Jews or I kill your little boy-soldiers. Only one set of children lives. It is your choice, not mine."

"You are crazy."

"No, I am practical. My hands are clean on the matter. It is your decision. Your way out of hell. It is either the lives of twenty young German men, the future of our country, or twenty young Jews, the scourge of the earth. I would think it should be an easy choice. Jews or Germans, Germans or Jews," he said, moving his palms up and down, weighing air like scales of justice until one scale, the one representing his idea of Germany, overwhelmed the other.

Heinrich moved in close to his friend, pulling his cheek next to Frederick's until they touched. The two men eyed the Jews lined in front of the chamber's door. He whispered, "Look at them, Frederick. They are so frail. So weak. To have come this far in their journey of life and die in such a hideous manner, they could never have imagined. Such a pitiful death. But you can end it quickly. Think of them as butterflies. Your coveted butterflies. You are doing nothing more than placing them in a poisoning jar, not to kill but to preserve for heaven. Do the thing. The right thing for Germany."

Frederick VonObst turned to look at his squad of soldiers and began to sob. "Remember this," he wailed. "I did this deed to save *your* lives. May God have mercy on my soul. May God have mercy on all of us here today."

He walked to the chamber door and opened it. Without saying anything, the children entered knowing exactly what to do. They ignored their executioners as they shuffled by, holding each other's hands and repeating the same passionless flight to death as their parents and grandparents.

Heinrich grinned broadly watching his friend usher in the children. He grinned even broader when the idea struck. Turning to the squad, he ordered them to sing at the top of their lungs, contending song would calm the children even more than

Brodifacoum. He insisted they sing *Lili Marlene*. And they obeyed, behaving like good soldiers, the way Sergeant Freddy had pledged they would on that first day:

> *Underneath the lantern by the barrack gate,*
> *Darling I remember the way you used to wait;*
> *'Twas there that you whispered tenderly,*
> *That you'd love me,*
> *You'd always be,*
> *My Lili of the lamplight,*
> *My own Lili Marlene . . . .*

Frederick closed the door behind the children and secured the latch. The remaining SS executioner opened one of two valves flooding the chamber with fumes. Frederick opened the second with the combined mixtures dealing a lethal blow. Frederick watched the murder through the peephole as the children's bodies twitched and convulsed, until the last of their gossamer limbs froze motionless. They were indeed like his butterflies, he thought, struggling for life until the very end, only to succumb to man.

"They are dead, Heinrich. Are you happy? Is there now enough blood spilled to please you?" He yelled.

"The only blood pleasing me now, Frederick, is the blood on your hands."

Frederick kicked the ground, shaking his fist. He no longer worried about Heinrich's threats. What remained important was getting his boys out of camp alive. He stood at the front of the squad, instructing them to make a tight formation, two abreast. Then, one last time, he marched them through camp, goose-stepping in perfect unison past the deserted barracks and the idled smokestacks and out of the prison that would live forever as a testament to man's nightmarish inhumanity to man. He escorted them to an abandoned checkpoint to safety and bid them farewell.

"Frederick, what are you still doing here?" Heinrich asked, bewildered by his presence. "I thought you had left."

Frederick said nothing at first and simply milled throughout the commandant's plush living quarters. He touched the paintings, felt the fabric on the lounging sofa, and fondled a Greek vase. He would miss the evenings he and Heinrich shared playing chess, talking philosophy, drinking schnapps. He once found the room a haven from the insanity of war. Now he realized it had merely served as a front for the real insanity. He sat opposite his leader and noticed the pistol resting on the table; a glass of peach schnapps lay half-consumed.

"I cannot leave," he finally uttered.

"Cannot leave? Nonsense. You must leave. The British are entering the valley as we speak. They will be here any minute. You do not want to be here when they pass those gates—trust me."

"But I do want to be here. Whatever happens to me, I deserve."

"No, Frederick. You are a good soldier. Go home."

"I am not a good soldier. How could I be? You see, I suspected—we all suspected—what was going on inside these walls but we chose to look the other way and ignore the killings. My apathy makes me an accomplice. It makes me as guilty as you, if for no other reason than for not stopping your kind. So, *I insist on staying*."

Heinrich sighed. "Well, maybe we should have one last drink together before I finish things here." He poured Frederick a full glass of schnapps, thrusting it into his friend's hand. "Here is to our children. The war may have been lost but not this one—not this one." He saluted his sergeant with the glass and downed the drink with one quick swallow. Next, he grabbed his pistol, cocked it, calmly placed it against his temple and pulled the trigger. The recoil snapped his head sideways, splattering blood and brains on the wall.

Frederick stared at the lifeless body sprawled in the chair with smoke pouring from the head. He put down his drink without consuming it. "I told you before, Heinrich, I would only drink with you *until* my conscience breaks—not after."

Stefan interrupted the trance.

"Frederick. Hurry. They are coming. We must leave. Come," he beckoned, waving his arm frantically.

"What are you doing here, Stefan?"

"I came to find you, my friend. I followed you here. The boys told me where they thought you would be. They told me everything. Now we must get you out of here at once."

Frederick shook his head. "I cannot leave. Do you not understand? I must pay for my sins. For Germany's sins. Leave me, Stefan, and never forget what went on in this place. *Never forget.*"

"But this is crazy. *Sins*? This is not your fault. You cannot blame yourself. What you are doing? Staying here is suicide. They will kill you for sure."

"Leave at once." Frederick barked. "That is an order,

private."

Stefan read the determination in Frederick's face, realizing any additional coaxing would only prove futile. He turned and walked away without looking back, following orders for the first time in his life.

(1972)

"Have you given up completely, this search to find your parents?" Zoey asked.

"I suppose," Richard answered. "The meeting yesterday just seemed phony. The entire time I had this funny feeling Mrs. VonObst wasn't leveling with me."

"Did you tell her who you are?"

"No. I should have but I didn't."

"Why not?"

"I wasn't sure she was the right woman. I panicked. Besides, I didn't trust her to tell me the truth."

"She was holding back? Hiding something?"?"

"Yes. The photos of her husband and all the other little things didn't add up. In fact, it was downright eerie. The man even resembled me—but twenty years older."

"That is all you have to go by? The look-alike photos?"

"No, there's more. Get this: When I asked her if she had any children she didn't say, 'No' or 'I have no children.' Her reply was, 'I have no son.' Now, don't you find her words a bit odd?"

"That is strange. Why would she have said 'no son'?" Zoey thought for a few seconds, speculating reasons. "Look, suppose she is your mother and she did give you up for whatever reason. Maybe, she did not want you back in her life. Maybe, the memory is too hard for her. Maybe, the memories are too traumatic," she stated. "I think you ought to call it quits, Richard."

"I can't."

"In that case, take the car, go back and confront her. Tell her who you are this time. Get everything out in the open."

Richard drove alone to Freiburg, not entirely sure how best to explain himself to the mysterious Lili VonObst. He felt awkward divulging his past in front of a stranger, especially if it turned out she was not the one whom he was hunting. He also realized this might be his last chance to discover the truth. Reluctantly, he tapped on her front door, hoping she might be at the store and he would not have to unload his weighty baggage.

Oscar immediately began barking, sniffing through the door's mail slot. Lili threw the door wide open.

"Richard, what a pleasant surprise. Back for tea?"

"That would be nice, Mrs. VonObst, but—"

"Please call me Lili. No one has called me *Mrs.* In years."

"Very well, Lili. If you have a few minutes, there's something I need to discuss with you. You see, I wasn't completely honest yesterday about who I am or why I came here to see you."

She drew a bewildered look on her face and motioned for him to come inside. He moved to the couch in the living room. Once again she sat opposite him in her stiff ladder-back chair.

"You mean our meeting yesterday was not necessarily by chance after all?" She asked.

"No. I deliberately came here for a reason."

"Well, I guess I should be honored. Is it my poetry? I understand it has been appearing in English editions in America. The University is notorious about doing things like that. Publishing our works. Telling us after-the-fact."

"To be honest, I didn't know you were a poet but I think that's great. I love poetry. Always have."

"*Oh*? Then, why are you here?"

"Because I need to find out something—*about myself*. I need to find out if you're my mother. You see, in 1946, I was abandoned as an orphan at a Red Cross camp not too far from Freiburg. From there my parents, my parents in America, adopted me. I was only three at the time and don't remember any of it. In fact, no one at the camp knew my age because no one knew who I was. I had no papers. No identity. My only possession was a glass shadow box strapped across my shoulders. It contained—"

"*Butterflies*."

"Yes. How did you know?"

She smiled uneasily. Her voice cracked. "Because those butterflies meant the world to your father. They were his life's work. It only seemed appropriate they should accompany you on your journey." With the admission she began to cry.

He fell back in the couch, mouth agape. Countless questions raced through his mind. With the train to Stuttgart scheduled to depart in two hours, there would be little time to get reacquainted. What to do next? What to say? But as he reflected on her choice of words he grew angry and erupted. "*My Journey?* How in the world would an abandoned three-year-old child know anything about journeys?" He barked.

"You were two."

"Fine. How was a two-year-old supposed to face the world alone on a journey?"

"There was no world for you to face here, in Germany, at least not as a VonObst."

"What do you mean? I had you. I had my father. Why would you both abandon me?"

"Your father didn't abandon you. It was all my doing."

"But why?" As he asked the question, he slid around the tea table separating them and knelt by her side. "<u>Why</u>?" He pursued.

"There are things best left unanswered, Richard. Let's just say I abandoned you so you could avoid the truth—*the ugly truth*—about the VanObsts. Is it not enough you lived in a wonderful country like the United States? That you were loved by good people and taught right from wrong? Why would you need anything more than what you have been given in life?"

"Because I have never felt complete without you. Your image never left this head," he whispered. "For twenty-six years I've dreamt of a woman who darted back and forth between my imagination and my childhood memories. Of a woman who loved me unquestionably because I was her son. Who rocked me to sleep at night. Who kissed me and told me how wonderful I was. I missed being told I was loved. *I missed you*."

He buried his head on her lap. She ran her fingers through his hair, stroking it softly.

"Don't cry little Jon-Jon. Please don't cry. I will tell you everything." And she began her story:

"It was the winter of 1946. Germany in the days after the war was a disaster. No one had food. There was no money. No currency. We had British pounds saved from before the war but when I ran out, I had nothing, absolutely nothing, for us to live on. Our world had turned upside down.

"We were very poor and very destitute. I was a struggling assistant at the university, left alone to raise you by myself. You had to sleep with me at night to stay warm. It was a bad winter." She shuddered at the recollection. "There were many nights you cried yourself to sleep because I could not feed you. I cannot tell you how tormented your weeping made me feel—*it drove me crazy with guilt*. Yes, that is it. I was crazy. I had to be to give you up and I had to give you up to feed you. You were all I had in the world. But I remembered how families in America loved German children. How they wanted to adopt our blue-eyed babies. I remembered how America was a place of opportunity and new beginnings. One day I decided to leave you at a Red Cross camp. They had food there. Lots of it. I knew they would not turn you away. I also knew if they could trace you to me, they would return you. So, I purposely gave you no identity, except for the shadow box with the butterflies, the one item your father treasured."

"But where was my father through all this? Why were you here by yourself after the war? Did he walk out?"

"It is best you not know."

"I must know. *I insist*."

"Very well," she replied, holding his hand. "No, he did not walk out on us. Freddy would never do that. He loved us but I am afraid he also loved his country—perhaps, too much, too blindly. You see, after the war he was put in prison. He was captured by the British at the Nazi-run extermination camp where he was stationed. He was accused of committing war crimes. They never could prove your father was involved but he willingly confessed to the brutal murder of at least twenty Jewish children and was hanged in 1949 by the tribunal in Nuremberg. He never told me why he committed such a grievous thing. I always found it difficult to believe he was capable of such horror. That was not the man I married. The man I married was a kind gentle soul who simply loved butterflies and his family.

"Sadly, no one came to his defense and no one had any sympathy for him at the trial. They would not even allow me to talk to him." She paused to reflect on the memory and in the process quit stroking her son's hair. "If the truth be known, that was my main reason for giving you up. I wanted you to have a new identity and not be haunted by a past with which you had no involvement. I asked myself how the son of Frederick VonObst could live in Germany without being despised. Why should you be shamed for your father's sins? So, I did what I thought best for you. I gave you a new life. Later, I had friends at the veteran's office destroy your father's court records. No one could ever link you to him. Whatever you achieved in life would be your own doing."

After her story, Richard stormed out of the house a troubled man and a doubting soldier. His mother was right—some things are best left undiscovered. If his true essence linked to his biological father's, it meant he, too, could be capable of committing unthinkable atrocities. History repeats, he told himself. It repeats unforgivingly. You cannot change genetic programming. You cannot change the essence of who you are. Remorsefully, he convinced himself that he could become a lethal time bomb waiting to explode, exactly as he had done on the train when he attempted to strike Zoey—Zoey, of all people. *What kind of animal could deliberately harm Zoey?* And instantly, intuitively, he knew he could never return to Vietnam. He could no longer trust himself. Like a string of dominos collapsing one upon the other, his thoughts collided. Distrust heralded self-doubts. Self-doubts brought anguish and anguish ushered the return to the abyss.

What to do next? He asked himself. Stay in hiding and disgrace the uniform? Seek refuge like a criminal? Not honor his military oath to the army? Or fight the damn war, fearing every step along the way a new ingredient, the ability to kill without remorse, would rear its head and with it the ugly truth about himself? The same endless debate—the same torment all over again as days before. These thoughts wore on him, beating his frail psyche and consuming him to the breaking point. Now, he simply needed to escape the never-ending madness.

"Gotta get some sleep . . . need sleep. . . ."

Racing the Porsche back to the cottage, he pressed harder on the accelerator. Speed helped him forget; it helped him cope. He felt wind running its fingers through his hair and soothing his soul the way his mother once did. The wind beckoned him to join it free of worries for eternity, free to journey through time and space like the butterflies he kept preserved all those years—*free to sleep forever.*

He had a conscience, he told himself, unlike his father. He knew right from wrong. And, yet, somewhere tempered between the harsh reality of righteousness and the cyclonic swirl of self-doubt, he reached a breaking point. Driving furiously to nowhere, he decided it best to end his life else risk becoming his father, becoming Frederick VonObst.

"Gotta sleep . . . need sleep. . . ."

When he reached the short curve in the road, the Porsche's speed exceeded one hundred fifty kilometers an hour. He must have known the centrifugal force surpassed the vehicle's capabilities. After all, he loved to race cars; he had grown intimately familiar with that particular vehicle. And he must have wanted to end up dead, wrapped around a sturdy spruce on the fringe of the meadow where he made love to Zoey. But by then he didn't care about living. He wanted his journey to end. He wanted to sleep.

(2000)

"Are we finished with the story, Mitchell?"

He wrinkled his nose, not quite sure how to answer the question—one of those simple questions the deliverer never appreciates can be sophisticatedly complex like 'What time is it?' and a timepiece scientist could only answer by explaining the complexities of the watch itself. He thought maybe she was playing a mind games with him, one of those thought provoking ink-blot tests set in the form of a question. And he decided not to fall prey to the trap and, instead, turned sideways on the couch to see what she was doing. She patiently stared back at him, awaiting his reply. Her pearl necklace dangled over the first draft of the new novel he had given her to read the night before.

"Beats catching you looking out the window," he mumbled sarcastically, deciding to sit up to address her face-to-face. "Gee, Laura, that's a toughie. When is a story ever finished? I mean, I think of my writings as works-in-progress, even if they've been submitted in final draft to the printer. You know, all the print does is capture the author's expression at a singular moment in time. My stories are sculptures molded in soft clay. You're constantly changing a little here, a little there, because you never realize the unattainable perfection you want in your mind—the unattainable perfection you want for the reader."

She raised her eyebrows. "Uh-huh. A simple 'Yes' or 'No' would have sufficed."

"Maybe for you but not for me. Look, a story ain't over *until the last period on the last page*."

"Okay. Are we on the last page? The last period?"

"What do you think?" He eyed the manuscript.

"No. I think we're close but there's still more to the story."

"Oh? And why do you say that?" He asked, somewhat miffed.

"Because, Mitchell, there are things in it I don't understand completely. I'm not sure if you even understand everything you've written. This thing's tragic. If you find it cathartic, may God have mercy on your soul."

He sneered. "Life's tragic *and tragedy sells*."

"But this story feels unfinished. There's something missing. Something lacking." She paused to reflect on her next question. "Where did the idea for these odd stories come from, anyway? They seem awfully personal."

"They are."

"In what way?"

"They're the answers to the lies. They're the *ugly truth*."

"Hm-m-m. When did you discover this so-called ugly truth."

He hesitated, thinking back to the beginning. "When my mother died two months ago."

"Go on. I'm all ears."

"When she died, I went through a trunk she kept hidden in the attic. My father didn't know what was in it, only that it needed to be cleaned out and he asked me to do it—all too painful for him. What I discovered were keys to my past. A past hidden from me. Lies about my *real* father and his father."

"The two men in your story?"

"Yes. You see, I didn't want to tell you about them until I finished writing the story. I wanted you to know the truth before we talked about them."

"Keep going."

"Alright. I was told when I turned eighteen my father, Arnold Jameson, was not my biological father. My mother remarried when I was eighteen months old and Arnold gave me his family name because my father had died a few months before. My mother said she divorced my real father because he was too in love with the military. That he was never home and had girlfriends. She said what ended it all was the discovery about one particular girlfriend in Freiburg. Someone named Zoey."

"That's not the way it plays in the book."

"I know, because the way it plays in the book is the closest I can come to the truth based on the research I did. You see, I think my mother lied to me about my real father and his father."

"And how did you uncover the supposed true versions?"

"The newspaper clippings she kept and the letters from officers serving with my father. My real father's adoption papers and the Internet."

"*The Internet?*"

"Yes. I discovered my grandfather on the Internet. In 1974, *Der Spiegel*, a German magazine, published a story titled, 'The Shame of Sergeant VonObst.' It was the confession of the survivors from his World War II squad, the soldiers who served under him. They finally admitted to the story I recounted in my book. By not coming forward at his trial in Nuremberg, they might as well have put the noose around his neck themselves. They could have prevented the whole thing. I decided my father, being a proud soldier, must have found out about Frederick VonObst, the supposed war criminal, when he was stationed in Germany. He must have been digging into the past, like me, trying to discover who the man really was. When he dug too deep, he uncovered a father who butchered children. The revelation must have tormented him. The fact he died outside Freiburg in a mysterious car accident in 1972, tells me he probably located his biological mother. She undoubtedly told him the story of his father, the only version she knew at the time. What he didn't know was the truth. As far as the girlfriend, I'm going by what my mother told me and a few letters. Most of it is conjecture."

"So there was really a Zoey?"

"There was a letter from a woman named Zoey addressed to my mother. The woman lived in Freiburg. I found the letter in the trunk. She had many kind things to say about my father and professed her love for him but I don't know for sure what went on."

"And you think your biological father deliberately killed himself that night—that he couldn't handle the idea his own father committed atrocities?"

"Yes. I think he was concerned with what was going on in Vietnam and the war atrocities we recognize today. I think when you add the pressure of the third tour, the wife who left him, and the supposed Nazi murderer father, he buckled. Such a waste."

"A waste?"

"He took the coward's way out. There are a multitude of things he could have done differently." He paused to collect his thoughts. "Shoot, Laura, there were a myriad of things both men could have done differently. But they opted to run away from their most important responsibility—their families."

"That seems to bother you, doesn't it? Not being able to make the right choice at a key juncture in your life? Beating yourself up when the decision is wrong."

"Yes."

"Well, you're not perfect, Mitchell. None of us are. Not your father. Not your grandfather."

"You can say that again."

"Why are you always hard on yourself?"

"Because I'm a fuck-up."

"No. We already dispelled that notion the first session. Remember?"

"Yeah. I remember *you* saying that."

Laura bit her lip as the thought occurred. "That's it, isn't it?"

"What's it?"

"You're afraid to forgive yourself. In a way, by writing this story, you were willing to forgive them and show compassion. It was okay for the great Mitchell Jameson to justify their actions but heaven forbid he should attempt to justify his own infidelity. And why is that?"

"Beats me."

"You know the answer. You're afraid to face the fact you're as human as they were. That you make mistakes like we all do. And you're scared aren't you?"

"Scared shitless."

"Why?"

"Because I don't want to become another tragic figure. I don't want to end up like them." He hesitated before turning his head away. "You don't get it, do you?"

"Get what?"

"What really happened. *The real situation*. When I found the trunk in the attic, I was already in the middle of the affair—into a full month of it with the other woman. I'd already decided to leave Susan and the girls. That was my decision. My stupendous choice. The trysts. The cheating. The infidelity. It all started *before* I discovered the trunk. Before I even knew of the VonObst legacy. The discovery and the ensuing research were my wake-up calls. Once I figured out the family pattern and the disastrous affects, that's when I decided to run off to Colorado and get away from everyone. The other woman—she was my wrong choice. And guess what? The infidelity coincided with the migration of butterflies. Now it was my turn to fuck-up. To follow in my predecessors footsteps—*right on schedule after twenty-eight years*."

Mitchell began to sob. Laura moved from behind her desk and embraced him.

"It doesn't matter *when* the decision happened. The truth is, Mitchell, none of this has to do with the migration of butterflies. It has to do with making a bad choice when you're most vulnerable. It means you're human and imperfect. And you know what the irony is?"

"What?"

"You're willing to make changes in your life so these kinds of mistakes don't happen again. But you're not willing to forgive yourself. How are you ever going to make it work with Susan if you can't do that?"

"I don't know."

"Look. Forgiveness is a grace we bestow on others to not only help them but to help us move on with our lives. It's a human way of letting go of the past. If we don't let go, we never find peace. We flounder. We stew. We suffocate. But, sometimes, the act of forgiveness also has to extend to ourselves. Without that self-realization we stumble. Without forgiving ourselves we remain lost. So, it begins with the words. It begins with the admission. And it's time for you to say it."

"You mean, *I forgive myself?*"

"Yes."

Mitchell fell back in the couch and stared at the floor. All the time spent alone in Colorado had as much to do with the guilt he had been unable to shed as with the actual act of infidelity. The marital infidelity he could never forget. It would always be there as a dark memory but to move forward he needed to forgive himself else the healing with Susan could never complete. It would remain an open sore festering for years. "I do forgive myself," he finally uttered. "I do. But. . . ."

"But what?"

"How do I ever get over the shame? How do I scrub away what I did?"

"You don't. You learn from your mistakes and put your best foot forward. Understand?"

"Yes, but it's painful."

"Yup. Always will be."

They remained silent for a full minute, Mitchell still staring at the floor, Laura's eyes affixed on Mitchell. Finally, Laura spoke. "I'd like to hear you say the words, again. I know you can do better than before. Say it this time like you mean it."

Mitchell took a deep breath. "I forgive myself."

"Keep going. Say it again with more conviction."

"I forgive myself," he said louder. After the words, a look of bewilderment swept over Mitchell's face. He glanced at Laura as the concept sunk in, when he fully grasped what she wanted him to realize. It was an epiphany long in the making. "I'm sorry I messed up," he stated slowly, "but I'm human and I'm. . . . I'm going to try to do things differently from now on to be a better person."

"Like what?"

"Like talk to Susan when I have worries. Seek professional help when I feel worthless. Pray when I need direction. And move on with my life, putting the past behind me."

She smiled. "You know something? It occurred to me that your reconciling with Susan has already been decided. Susan wants you back. You want it to work. Seems to me, your marriage has been given a second chance. Sometimes marriages that go through these things actually come out stronger."

He tried to reciprocate the smile. "How's all this going to end, Laura?"

"It's entirely your call. You won't know *until the last period on the last page*. Remember? That's what you told me."

"Up to me, huh?"

"Yup, but I think it would help if you cast aside some ghosts."

"Ghosts? You mean the VonObst legacy. The other screw ups?"

"I'm not sure they did screw up. It seems to me your grandfather was a very honorable man and loved his family. Maybe he shouldn't have left Lili and the baby the summer of 1944, but I'm not convinced his decision was necessarily wrong. He did what he thought was the right thing to do. It just happened to be a journey with a tragic ending.

"Truth is you don't really know what happened to your biological father that August of 1972. In your mind you've created an illusion to deal with the bits and pieces of what you discovered in the trunk and on the Internet. Remember what we talked about the other night at the club? Remember what you told me? You said that illusions help us cope. The truth is illusions are deceivers. They postpone the inevitable reality of our lives.

"And one other thing, choices aren't necessarily tied to our *genetic programming,* contrary to your thinking," she stated, repositioning to sit on the corner of her desk. "That's the difference between us and butterflies. They're instinct driven. We are not. We have consciences. Free will determines our fate. The question is: are you strong enough to cast aside illusions, this imaginary link to the twenty-eight year migration of butterflies?"

"I think I'm ready but what reality is there left to face?"

"The truth about your biological father."

"How?"

"By confronting your demons. I think you should go to Germany. Take the next flight. Find this Lili VonObst and get answers straight from her. Decide for yourself if there's any validity to the illusion you've created," she said, hesitating for a brief moment. "And—"

"And what?"

"And decide once and for all if it was fate guiding your father's actions or free will. Once you have laid to rest that last question, you'll be in a better position to determine your future."

EIGHT
(2000)

Tracking down Lili VonObst's whereabouts proved easy enough. She still lived in the Bavarian-styled bungalow outside Freiburg, the one she and Frederick spent a year of their lives together in. She retired a full professor with the University of Freiburg thirteen years earlier as a senior chairperson in the Department of International Literature. Since retirement she had spent her days doing what she loved most—reading and writing poetry. Nearing eighty years old, she was no longer able to venture far from home or climb the steep hill from town, with her outings restricted to grocery store Mondays. She led a lonely and solitary life waiting for the day she would be reunited with Freddy. With few friends alive and no relatives, her only companion had been a stray dog she adopted a few years earlier. The dog had no name and slept most of the time on her front porch.

When the taxi pulled up to the house and the young man with the GAP ball cap climbed out, she had no idea who he was. Visitors had been a rarity. She peered through curtain windows at the stranger, unsure whether or not to answer the doorbell. Yet, even with his unusual foreign bearing, she felt compelled to open the door.

"Woher kommst du? (Where do you come from?)" She asked, from behind the door.

"Look, I'm awfully sorry but I don't speak a word of German."

"It is quite all right," she replied. "I speak English. Are you from Texas?"

"Why, yes. How did you know?"

"I know my American dialects. Years of teaching made me proficient at deciphering them."

"I'm impressed." He smiled. "Very impressed."

"Thank you."

He removed his backpack and held out his hand, thrusting it through the crack of the door. "My name is Mitchell Jameson. I've come all the way from the States to meet you, Mrs. VonObst."

She smiled and shook his hand, puzzled why anyone would come from America to meet her. "Do I know you?" She pursued.

"Probably not, but you probably know or *knew* my father," he stammered, flustered by the question. "Would it be possible for me to come inside? It's been a long journey."

"Of course. Come. Come." She signaled him to follow her.

He threw the backpack over a shoulder and hopped over the dog. The pace inside, however, moved much slower behind her laborious gait as she manipulated a walker and scooted it across the wooden floor to the living room.

"I am as slow as a turtle these days. It is the hip. I lost significant joint movement a few years back. I am awfully sorry."

"No. No, that's fine. Really," he reassured.

She pointed to a sofa in the corner. "Have a seat on the couch, Mitchell. I am going to start tea for us and, then, I will return."

He watched her shuffle into the kitchen and around the corner and out of sight. It gave him time to study the house. The place seemed nothing like what he imagined. There were no shrines to Frederick VonObst, no stacked photographs lining shelves and nooks, no piano crammed in a corner with framed snapshots, no memorabilia or remembrances strewn anywhere. On the contrary, the room appeared Spartan and tidy with ample maneuvering clearance for a walker. If Frederick VonObst had ever lived there, no one would know. As he continued to size-up the place, he removed his cap and twirled it nervously in his hands. He could hear her movements in the next room—water splashing the insides of a tea kettle, a crisp metallic clang as she refitted the lid, a gas hiss and pop on the stove, and the walker scuffing the floor as she returned.

"Oh, good. I am glad you are comfortable. The tea should be ready in a few minutes," she stated, pulling herself nearer. "You do drink tea. Yes?"

"Yes. I sure do. Usually with ice," he stammered again. "We Texans are ice tea lovers, you know."

"Yes, I do know. I spent a summer internship at the university in Austin twenty years ago. I had to work very hard at finding restaurants serving hot tea."

She stopped short of the couch, positioned herself sideways and let go of the walker, collapsing beside him. He slid over to give her more room.

"Austin, huh?" He exclaimed. "What a coincidence. I'm from Austin. I've lived there my entire life but haven't been home in a few months."

"And why is that?" She asked.

"I've been in Colorado. Vail. It's a ski resort."

"That is a pleasant place, too." She smiled. "But why have you been living in Colorado?" She could tell the question made him uncomfortable. "Are you okay?" She asked.

"Yes. I'm fine. I've been living there because my wife and I have been separated."

"*Oh?*"

"It's a long story. We've had some problems and, well, it won't be forever. We've got these two beautiful girls and—"

She put her hand on his knee, stopping him mid-sentence. "Mitchell, it is none of my business. I am sorry."

"No, it's alright. Really." He laughed nervously. "Actually, it is more than alright."

"Go on," she encouraged.

"You see, the reason I'm here is because you are part of my marriage therapy. You are a link to my past."

"You mean, to the man you mentioned earlier, your father?"

"Yes."

"And what link would that be?"

He looked away for a few seconds, working up enough courage to tell her the truth. "My father was Richard O'Malley—*your son.*"

Her eyes widened. As her mouth fell open, she instinctively raised her hand to cover it, astonished by the announcement. Then, she broadcast a wide expressive grin and nodded her head. "So, you are Richard's Mitchell. I should have known. You are the spitting image of him. Almost as handsome, too. He showed me pictures of you when you were a year old. I am so happy we finally get to meet." She threw her arms around her grandson.

Taken aback by her reaction, it took Richard a few seconds to reciprocate the embrace. "You actually knew my father?"

"Yes. My son and I became reacquainted when he was

stationed in Stuttgart in 1972. He visited me all the time. Every free weekend he would race his Porsche here."

"I had no idea. I wasn't even completely sure you two ever met. There was no record of it and I assumed—"

"*It was our secret*. You see, in those days we were all led to believe his father, your grandfather, was a murderer. That he was an accomplice at the Bergen-Belsen concentration camp. Your father never believed it, though. Not for one second. I don't know why your father had such a strong conviction about the matter. He always said how anyone with a gentle love for butterflies could never murder human beings. How it ran counter to their temperament. He read all the letters your grandfather wrote me during the war. He kept all the photographs. Did all the research," she paused. "He started it all, you know."

"*Started what?*"

"The crusade. The fight to clear your grandfather's name. Your father came to Freiburg and did research at the veterans' office. He is the one who found the names of the boys who served under your grandfather during the war. He is the one who started the letter writing campaign and who discovered the truth. His initiative got the article published in *Der Spiegel* a few years later. He even had to steal war records to prove it."

Mitchell fell back against the sofa, lost in thought. "My mother told me he came to Freiburg to visit a girlfriend. Someone named Zoey."

She laughed. "Zoey? My goodness, that is me—*I am Zoey*."

"I don't understand," he pursued, shaking his head.

"After your father and I became reacquainted, I made him

promise me he would not tell anyone I was his mother. I did not want his name linked to the notorious Frederick VonObst. If anyone ever discovered the connection, his distinguished military career could cease. After all, that is why I gave him up for adoption in the first place. To be clear of the VonObst atrocity. We invented a code name for me. He called me *Zoey*. Whenever we wrote each other, I always used my code name."

"And the night he died. I heard he was distraught. Out of his mind. He refused to return to Vietnam."

"Refused to return to Vietnam? No, not at all. The night he died was the same day he discovered the truth about your grandfather saving his young soldiers from that crazy butcher at Bergen-Belsen. He learned your grandfather had been extorted into killing twenty Jewish children to save twenty German boys' lives. No, your father became ecstatically happy that day and he celebrated the occasion. He drank a little too much. Drove a little too fast. *It was just an accident.* The road was slippery. It had been raining earlier in the day. He was actually looking forward to his third tour. He was, how do you say, gung ho. That was his nature. He loved the military."

Mitchell stared at the floor. "It's all so different from what I imagined. I thought my mother and he split because of girlfriends."

"I never met your mother. I wrote her once but as far as I know, she never knew the truth about me being his mother." She hesitated, noting his concern. "Mitchell, let me assure you, your father's only *girlfriend* was the military. Like his father, war was a lethal mistress. Perhaps, your mother created an illusion in her mind to help justify the divorce. We all do that, you know—create illusions to help us cope with life's harsh realities."

Mitchell buried his face in his hands. "My God, what have I done? What have I been doing all these months?"

Lili failed to completely understand his anguish but did sense his pain. She patted his back, ran her fingers through his hair. "There, there. It is okay, Mitchell. It is okay. Sometimes lies tear at our soul more than the truth. For years I lived in fear of the lies about your grandfather. It took your father to make me see the truth. Can you imagine what a long and difficult journey he had to go through to grow up in Iowa and find his way back to his home in Germany? Think about it. It took my son's unquestioned love to help me reaffirm love for my own husband," she stated, waiting a few seconds before continuing. "So, what is your excuse? Why this long journey of yours?"

"I don't understand?" He asked.

"I mean, your father and your grandfather each had wars separating them from loved ones. You have no war, Mitchell, except for the one here," she said, pointing to her head, "and in here." She touched her heart. "So, what is your excuse?"

He said nothing, being lost in thought, trying to rationalize all the shallow excuses he had made for leaving Susan.

"Mitchell, do you love your wife?"

"Yes."

"Then, why are you here? Why were you in Colorado? Go home to her in Texas. Go home to her right now. Your journey should be with her. Life is far too short to not share it with the ones you love most."

He stood, nodding his head in agreement. "You're right. It is time for me to go home. It's been long overdue. I should never have left her. In fact, would it be alright if I bring my family back here to meet you?"

"Oh, my goodness. *Yes*. I would enjoy that very much."

He bent over, kissed her on the cheek, and threw the backpack over a shoulder. "You don't have to see me out. And you'll definitely hear from me in a few days."

His mind raced with the newfound knowledge causing him to almost forget the gift he brought. Halfway to the door, he unzipped the backpack and rummaged until he found the item. "Here. This is for you." He handed her the gift—the glass shadow box with two rare butterflies, Old World Swallowtails, mounted on its backboard. "I believe this belongs to you. I found it with a stash of things in a trunk in my mother's attic."

She held it at arm's length and squinted to read the inscription in the corner. When she realized its origin, she was unable to contain her emotion. *"This is wonderful.* Absolutely wonderful, Mitchell. Why, I remember the day your grandfather caught these two. I remember like it was yesterday. He was so proud. So pleased with himself. We both hoped this day would come, when I could tell our grandchildren about the event. When you come back, I'll relive for you that glorious day in August of 1944. Such a joyous reunion." She sighed staring at the lifeless butterflies. "You know, in a way, it is a shame."

"What's a shame?" He asked.

"That we cannot set them free."

Mitchell smiled softly, thinking about her words. Before he closed the door, he turned one last time to bid farewell. "Maybe we have set them free, *Grandmother*." Reluctantly, he waved good-bye.

After Mitchell left, Lili decided to steal to the dining room, her post-retirement office. The shadow box tucked under one arm while she scooted in the walker. On the way, she stopped by a record player and searched for a song, one she had not played in years. When she found the right album, she laid it on the turntable, accidentally bouncing the ceramic needle off the record's worn grooves. Fortunately, the music forgave her. Soon, it filled the house with the lyrics of her favorite song, *Lili Marlene*. The tune sounded scratchy, exhausted by countless listening, but the melody and words remained lucid. She grinned remembering how Freddy used to sing the song in her ear, off-key but heartfelt. She could even hear his voice, she thought, and decided to hum in unison.

When she sat by the table and laid the box on its side, she noticed a compressed wad of paper dropping to the floor, bouncing off the walker's aluminum struts. The wad had been wedged in the backside of the wooden frame but somehow jarred loose. She struggled to pick it up; eventually, she snared it and unfolded the brittle parchment. The paper had yellowed with time but the ink still read legibly. It was the unfinished poem started years before. She smiled with the recollection and the inspiration Freddy once kindled in the meadow behind their house the day the butterflies returned in 1944. And she read the poem aloud:

> *I watched you sleeping again last night,*
> *so far away in slumber's arms,*
> *dreaming about your fields of butterflies.*
> *And as I watched, I softly touched your face,*
> *caressing your skin, smelling your hair,*
> *my senses lost in you.*

Then, I, too, dreamed—
dreamed of us making love,
with love making so deliciously sweet,
the taste of your lips against mine
stirred my soul.
And I asked myself:
How shall I live without you by my side?
How shall I live without you?

The answer seemed obvious, she thought. She grabbed a fountain pen and immediately began writing:

With steadfast love.
When two devoted hearts unite,
their souls begin an endless flight,
like the butterflies of Toulon,
always returning to heaven's gate.

With the poem completed, she folded the paper and wedged it back in the corner of the shadow box.

"There, Freddy. There is our answer," she proclaimed.

The shrill whistle of a steaming tea pot interrupted her tranquil moment. *Tea time.* She arose from the table and scooted toward the kitchen. Afternoon tea had become an integral part of her daily routine—her most favorite routine. She smiled recollecting the day's events and the discovery of her lost American family. But she grinned widest about the awaiting treat in the kitchen. Her pace quickened. She had always relished afternoon tea. Indeed, she adored her tea but not nearly as much as making love to Freddy on those balmy

Sunday afternoons in the summer of 1944.

When the telephone began to chirp, taunting him one last time, Mitchell was heading out the front door. The sixteen-hour drive back to Austin would be exhausting and he eagerly wanted to arrive home before sunset. He pivoted to curse the high-tech contraption. "Damn it. Why can't you frigging ting-a-ling?" Dropping his backpack on the floor, he sprinted to the phone before it had a chance to squawk a third time. Maybe the caller was Susan. He smashed the speakerphone button.

"*Hello*."

"Well, buddy boy, I got the manuscript. I like the changes."

"Thanks, Harvey. Look, can I call you back tomorrow? I'm in a rush."

"Sure. No problem. I just have one final question for you."

"Make it quick."

"Did our protagonist and his wife ever reunite? I mean, you didn't send the final chapter."

Mitchell's voice softened. "It's in the mail. The final chapter is in the mail, Harvey. Look for it tomorrow."

"But did they get back together? I need to know."

"Of course they did. Know what else?"

"What?"

"They lived happily ever after."

Harvey exhaled a long overdue breath. "You know something? I like that ending, buddy boy. I like it a lot. So, I guess our story is finally finished?"

"Yup. Down to the last period on the last page."

.

Other David Martin Anderson books
available through Amazon:

The Last Good Horse - Paperback ISBN 978-1-892617-16-3

Digital   ISBN 978-1-892617-17-0

Promises   - Paperback ISBN 978-1-892617-22-4

Digital   ISBN 978-1-892617-23-1

Harry's Apology   - Paperback ISBN 978-1-892617-15-6

Digital   ISBN 978-1-892617-19-4

Beaty Butte   - Paperback ISBN 978-1-892617-26-2

Digital   ISBN 978-1-892617-27-9